Tonight she was more aware than usual of her boss.

It was no surprise that she'd had a bit of a crush on him over the years. Alex was virile, lean and muscular. Even in the expensive suits he wore, his physical power was evident. Thick black hair, cut conservatively, and deep brown eyes added up to an extremely masculine and sexy man.

The longer she knew him, the more she was afraid he would pick up on her reluctant attraction.

She had no illusions on that score. Maria was practical and ambitious. She would get ahead by virtue of hard work and innate talent. But once in a while, she let herself fantasize about sharing Alex's bed. Thankfully, Alex was oblivious to her imagination.

She'd seen the hint of disapproval in his gaze tonight as he assessed her party dress. Why, she couldn't say. By Miami standards, her outfit was practically tame.

And she couldn't put a finger on what bothered her about his interaction with Gabriel Montoro. Instead of being conciliatory and cajoling to the prince, he'd been borderline antagonistic.

It made no sense.

Minding Her Boss's Business

JANICE MAYNARD

This is a work of fiction. Names, characters, places,
locations and incidents are purely fictional and bear no
relationship to any real life individuals, living or dead, or
to any actual places, business establishments, locations,
events or incidents. Any resemblance is entirely
coincidental.

First published in Great Britain 2015
by Mills & Boon, an imprint of Harlequin (UK) Limited,
Large Print edition 2015
Eton House, 18-24 Paradise Road,
Richmond, Surrey, TW9 1SR

© 2015 Harlequin Books S.A.

Special thanks and acknowledgment are given to
Janice Maynard for her contribution to the
Dynasties: The Montoros miniseries.

ISBN: 978-0-263-26036-6

Harlequin (UK) Limited's policy is to use papers that
are natural, renewable and recyclable products and made
from wood grown in sustainable forests. The logging
and manufacturing processes conform to the legal
environmental regulations of the country of origin.

Printed and bound in Great Britain
by CPI Antony Rowe, Chippenham, Wiltshire

JANICE MAYNARD

is a *USA TODAY* bestselling author who lives in beautiful east Tennessee with her husband. She holds a BA from Emory and Henry College and an MA from East Tennessee State University. In 2002 Janice left a fifteen-year career as an elementary school teacher to pursue writing full-time. Now her first love is creating sexy, character-driven, contemporary romance stories.

Janice loves to travel and enjoys using those experiences as settings for books. Hearing from readers is one of the best perks of the job! Visit her website, janicemaynard.com, and follow her on Facebook and Twitter.

For little girls everywhere
who dream of being princesses:
This one's for you…

One

Alex Ramon winced as shards of pain lanced his temples. Though the splitting headache was undoubtedly a result of jet lag and too little sleep for the past couple of weeks, it could also be attributed to stress. At the moment, his particular stressor stood on the opposite side of the room… a tall, leggy blonde in a formfitting aquamarine dress and killer heels.

Maria Ferro. Aged twenty-seven. Straight, honey-colored hair that tumbled like a silky waterfall almost to her ass. He probably shouldn't be thinking about her ass. Definitely not. But tonight it was difficult not to notice.

Reluctantly, he dragged his attention from

his coworker and surveyed the room. By all accounts, the party was going swimmingly. The delegation of business leaders from the European island nation of Alma mingled with the various members of the Montoro family, everyone chatting with animation and cordiality.

The ballroom was situated on the ground floor of one of Miami's premier hotels. An entire wall of glass showcased the azure ocean. Priceless chandeliers cast sparkles across the polished hardwood floor. The decor was understated, modern and sophisticated. Much like the wealthy Montoro family themselves.

Alex inserted a finger beneath the collar of his tux and tugged. He was more than accustomed to upscale social functions. But in this moment, restlessness plagued him. As Alma's deputy prime minister of commerce, he carried the lion's share of the responsibility for convincing the Montoros to return to their homeland and resume the throne.

A lot was riding on tonight and the days to come.

This evening's soiree was only the beginning... a chance for the delegation to be introduced and to establish personal contact with the family whose ancestors once ruled Alma. Unfortunately, the men and women in the youngest generation, all twenty-somethings, were more interested in hard-driving business deals and hard-partying social lives than in resurrecting any royal roots.

A throaty laugh echoed across the room. Maria was clearly enjoying her handsome companion. Gabriel Montoro, middle child of Rafael III, epitomized the classic bad boy...fun loving, hard to pin down, heedless of anyone's opinion. Alex wanted to dismiss him as a lightweight player, but in fact, Gabriel ran the South American division of Montoro Enterprises with surprising success. He was headquartered in Miami, which meant he would be involved in the upcoming negotiations.

Alex was surprised that the usually sensible Maria didn't see through Gabriel's facade. Perhaps she was blinded by the man's green eyes, tousled hair and golden skin. Alex wasn't jealous. That would be ludicrous. He and Maria were nothing more than business associates. But he was half a dozen years older than she was, and he felt protective of her.

She had worked for his family in London. Then, when political power changed hands in Alma and the Ramons were able to return to their homeland, Maria had come, as well, along with her mother. Alex had watched with satisfaction as Maria's talent and hard work brought opportunities her way. Now, as a marketing and PR expert, she was set to play an integral role in this new venture.

Alex admired and respected Maria. She was too nice a woman to be taken in by a jaded playboy like Gabriel Montoro.

Decades had passed since the last Montoro monarch was deposed by a dictator in the aftermath of the Second World War. Four generations later the family enjoyed the fruits of a shipping and trade empire that spanned half the globe.

The Montoros were happy and successful in Miami…legendary for their wealth and lifestyle. Only time would tell if they could be persuaded by duty and honor to walk a different path.

Alex made his way around the perimeter of the room, stopping to make introductions and to chat with this person and that. In his hotel room he possessed lengthy dossiers on each of the key players in tonight's drama. Though he had glanced over his notes before coming downstairs, the information was stored in his brain.

That was how he worked. Prepare for every eventuality. Plan for any outcome. Make no mistakes.

At last he reached the small alcove where Maria and Gabriel stood. She held a glass of wine in one hand, though Alex hadn't seen her drink more than a few sips. Gabriel Montoro appeared to be offering her naughty vignettes about their fellow partygoers.

Deliberately, Alex took his place at Maria's side and gave Montoro a steady glance. "Mr. Montoro. I'm Alex Ramon."

Gabriel nodded as the two of them shook hands. "I know. My father speaks highly of you. I have to tell you, though, you may have your work cut out for you. None of us are particularly interested in playing dress up with crowns and thrones and an antiquated system that has seen its day."

Alex rubbed a hand across his chin, hoping to defuse the awkward moment with humor. "Why don't you tell me what you're *really* thinking?" The man's blunt honesty caught him off guard.

Gabriel shrugged. "I'm not sure what all of you hope to gain."

Maria shot Alex a glance as if to caution tact. But Alex was off his game. And irritated. "Alma is in the midst of important changes. Restoring the monarchy in a ceremonial role is a popular idea with the people at large. The offshore oil reserves have made the country wealthy, but we need stability. A royal marriage would ensure that."

Gabriel's smile was mocking. "How very feudal of you, Mr. Ramon."

"This is not something to joke about. The lives and well-being of thousands of people are at stake here. Your family's history is part and parcel of Alma's identity."

Gabriel shook his head. "They threw us out with nothing but the clothes on our backs."

Alex shoved his hands in his pockets. He had the most insane urge to throttle the guy. Wouldn't that be a royal mess… "They didn't throw *you* out," he said, the words even. "You weren't even born. And the people had no say in it. You know what Tantaberra was like. He'd shoot first and ask questions later."

Gabriel shrugged. "Whatever. The point is, if you're trying to make my family and me face up to some kind of obligation, you're way off course. We have a good life here in Miami. Why would we want to return to a tiny backwater collection of islands that time forgot?"

Maria spoke up, her blue-green eyes sparkling with passion. "Alma has changed, Mr. Montoro. We have high-speed broadband internet access, satellite television and radio and a thriving business community. Along with the natural beauty of the land, we have much to offer."

Gabriel wasn't convinced. "I can find all that and more here in the US."

Alex played his trump card. "But think of your aunt…you know what she wants…"

A flicker in the other man's eyes told Alex he'd finally scored a point. Isabella, at seventy-three, was the oldest living Montoro. It was her dearest wish that her grandchildren, grandnieces and grandnephews return to their homeland for the sake of family honor. She was dying…caught up in the advanced stages of Parkinson's disease. Alex had a notion she was hanging on only long enough to see the transfer of power take place.

Gabriel downed the last of his champagne and plucked another crystal flute from the tray offered by a passing waiter. "Aunt Isabella lives in the past. We do not always get what we want."

"I think that's a song," Maria said, smiling. Clearly she was trying to lighten the mood. But Alex was in no frame of mind to be appeased. Gabriel Montoro rubbed him the wrong way. The man had wealth, power, good looks and sex appeal. It was rumored that women besieged him all hours of the night and day. Surely Maria wouldn't be so naive as to be taken in by him.

Gabriel sipped his drink, his gaze stormy. "Lucky for you, my father retains some vestige of the old ways. Perhaps he can be persuaded. Who knows?"

Alex winced, as did Maria. Maria laid a hand on Montoro's arm briefly, as if to placate him. "I think no one has told you," she said softly. "But your father cannot reign."

"Why the hell not?"

It was oddly amusing that even though Gabriel insisted his family had no interest in the monarchy, he was incensed at the notion his father was ineligible.

Alex took a deep breath and exhaled. "Your father is divorced. His marriage was not annulled. Under the tenets of Alma law, that legally disqualifies him."

"Hell of a way to operate a country. You should be damn glad I'm not in the running. If a man of my father's caliber is not on the short list, I'd never make the cut." The sarcasm was laced with disdain.

"This isn't personal, Mr. Montoro. We're merely trying to follow the traditions and expectations of our people."

Maria nodded. "Alex is right, of course. The situation is unprecedented. We are trying our best to make it work."

"But neither of you even lived in Alma until Tantaberra was ousted. Why do you care?"

Alex remained silent, unable to give voice to the emotions roiling inside him. Fortunately, Maria was more vocal. "Alex's family met the same fate as yours long ago, Gabriel. They, however, settled in London and rebuilt their fortunes in oil and gas. When Tantaberra was finally overthrown, Alex's father determined that returning to Alma was the right thing to do."

Gabriel shook his head, draining the second glass of champagne. "I seem to be surrounded by proponents of duty above desire. Thank God, my brother is the one in the hot seat. You'll never find a more honorable man. But whether or not he's interested in a crown remains to be seen."

Alex took Maria's elbow in a loose grip. "If you'll excuse us, Mr. Montoro, Maria and I need to mingle. I'm sure we'll meet again."

Gabriel eyed both of them, his rueful smile half apology, half derision. "I'm sure we will. How long do you anticipate staying in Miami to stir the pot?"

"A month, give or take. We have a great deal of work to do. The official request from Alma to the Montoro family is in the process of being drafted."

Maria spoke up. "And I'll be working on press releases and rollouts to the public. We want everything to be positive and upbeat."

"And if my family refuses?" Gabriel's steely-eyed gaze held not a whit of humor.

It was Alex's turn to shrug. "If your brother agrees, the rest of you will be free to make your own choices. Although, for the sake of a smooth transition, your support will mean a lot to him, I would think."

Maria grimaced. "This is a huge undertaking, Mr. Montoro."

"I asked you to call me Gabriel," he said. "And you, too, Alex. I'm not one to stand on ceremony." If he was making a point, it was subtle.

"Gabriel, then," she said. "We take our charge very seriously. I hope you'll give us a chance to win you over."

He chuckled. "Fair enough."

His relaxed response sent a wave of relief crashing through Alex. It would be bad form to alienate one of the royal family right out of the gate. Gabriel had been pissed a moment ago, but his tone and demeanor were mellower now.

"I appreciate your plain speaking," Alex said, his customary diplomacy back in working order. "I'll look forward to continuing our conversation."

Maria allowed Alex to steer her away from the Montoro bad boy, but for once, she couldn't read her boss. He led her toward the buffet. "Have you eaten anything?" he asked gruffly.

Her stomach rumbled on cue. "No. I was too nervous."

He handed her a plate. "We've both been working nonstop for weeks. I think we deserve a break."

Maria surveyed the bounty with anticipation. Fresh seafood, everything from shrimp cocktail to crab legs to raw oysters, filled silver trays to overflowing. The various salads and breads were no less appealing.

She made her choices and followed Alex to a small table for two. The glass doors were designed to be open for access to the patio, but it was much too hot at the moment for anyone to go outside.

She sat down, tugging the hem of her dress to a decorous level. Alex was in an odd mood. In a tiny pocket she carried a tube of lipstick and a small vial of tablets. Shaking two ibuprofen into her palm, she handed them across the table. "Your head is killing you, I can tell. Take these."

He scowled but didn't argue. She knew that men in general and this one in particular hated showing weakness of any kind. It was a sign of his discomfort that he didn't refuse.

They ate in silence for long minutes. The quiet didn't bother Maria. She'd grown up without brothers or sisters and had often spent time alone at home when her mother was at work.

Tonight, however, she was more aware than usual of her boss. It was no surprise that she'd had a bit of a crush on him over the years. Alex was virile, lean and muscular. Even in the expensive suits he wore, his physical power was evident. Thick black hair, cut conservatively, and deep brown eyes added up to an extremely masculine and sexy man.

In London, she had worked as his secretary. Once they all returned to Alma, however, she had been promoted to her current assignment in media and PR. Her position fell under the auspices of the Ministry of Commerce, but she did not ordinarily answer directly to Alex. For this assignment, however, he was definitely in charge. And that was a problem. Because the longer she knew him, the more she was afraid he would pick up on her reluctant attraction.

She had no illusions on that score. Alex was the eldest son of an aristocratic Alma family. He would marry one day and marry well. But not someone like Maria. Not a woman whose mother had been a laundress in a seedy neighborhood in London to make ends meet.

Maria was practical and ambitious. She would get ahead by virtue of hard work and innate talent. But, once in a while, she let herself fantasize about sharing Alex's bed. All that hard muscle and warm skin at her disposal. A shiver snaked its way from the nape of her neck to a spot low in her belly. Thankfully, Alex was oblivious to her imagination.

He was discreet about his relationships. A very private man with a fine-tuned sense of propriety. She'd seen the hint of disapproval in his gaze tonight as he assessed her party dress. Why, she couldn't say. By Miami standards, her outfit was tame.

Nevertheless, she knew she had blotted her copybook with Alex. Perhaps he thought her décolletage was too low or her skirt too high. Though the man was incredibly appealing, even she could admit he had a stuffy side. Perhaps she would have teased him had he not looked so grim faced. It occurred to her that he took this venture very personally. As if it was solely up to him to convince the Montoros to accept the mantle of the monarchy once again.

By the time they'd finished eating, the lines at the corners of Alex's mouth had disappeared. Between the food and the painkillers, he seemed finally to have relaxed. Still, she couldn't put a finger on what bothered her about his interaction with Gabriel Montoro. Instead of being conciliatory and cajoling, he'd been borderline antagonistic.

It made no sense.

She sipped a glass of Chablis and gazed out over the diverse group of people. The Alma delegation actually outnumbered the Montoros, but the Montoros had invited numerous friends and associates.

Rafael Montoro III was the life of the party. His rugged features belied his age. Though he had already turned fifty, he could pass for a man a decade younger. Did he harbor resentment over being bypassed for the throne?

His oldest son, Rafael IV—known as Rafe— was charming and affable and extremely self-possessed, though he had yet to hit thirty. Except for his age, it was not a stretch to see him as king of Alma. Rafe's sister, Bella, was much like her dad, the center of attention and a vivacious extrovert. But she was very young, only twenty-three if Maria remembered correctly.

Then there was Gabriel, who was another story. And also a close cousin, Juan Carlos, who had been raised with the Montoro siblings after his parents' deaths. Neither Gabriel nor Juan Carlos would be likely to play much of a role in the upcoming transition, except for supporting Rafael IV.

The others present were of little interest at this point. It would be Maria's job to craft the image of a royal family that was strong and moral and charismatic. The only person who might make her job difficult was Gabriel. Who knew what skeletons were hidden in *his* closet. It would be up to her to excavate them and make sure they didn't embarrass the Montoro family in the midst of this sea change.

Gabriel, despite his reputation, was not so bad, as far as she could tell. Perhaps a bit cynical, almost definitely a player. Women were always drawn to that kind of fallen-angel mystique.

"I don't know how this is going to go."

She jumped when Alex spoke. She'd been so deep in her thoughts he had startled her. She searched his face. "I've never heard you give voice to the possibility that we might not prevail."

His lips twisted. "Well, look at them. Why do they need Alma or royal titles? The whole family is practically royalty here in the States. If you or I were in their shoes, would we give up all this?"

"Maybe. It's hard to say." Maria pursed her lips. "Everyone likes knowing where he or she comes from. The Montoros' family history goes back hundreds of years. I imagine that once they have some time to think about it they'll be excited about renewing those ties."

"I hope you're right."

At the opposite end of the room, a small orchestra began tuning up. When the musicians launched into their first song, Alex stood and held out his hand. "Do you feel like dancing?"

Her heart fluttered and lifted. "I *always* feel like dancing."

As he led her out onto the floor, she tried not to stiffen up. That would be a dead giveaway that she was nervous.

Alex held her firmly with masculine confidence that was appealing. She was a strong, capable woman, but to move like this… Well, that was another thing entirely. Here she could give in to the mastery of the dance. Alex was in charge, and she was able to let go and let him steer their course.

He smelled of crisp, starched cotton and warm male skin. She was almost certain she caught a whiff of the hotel's signature shower gel. Her heart pounded in her chest, and her knees trembled. This was the first time they had ever been so close.

In Alma, she couldn't think of a single social occasion when she and Alex had interacted so personally. And for such a length of time. Perhaps that was why she felt a change in him.

The first song ended and a second began. Alex made no move to release her. Since she had no real desire to *be* released, she followed where he led. A less pragmatic woman might have called the moment romantic. Maria was neither a romantic nor a wishful thinker. But even a realist could choose to live in the moment once in a while.

Life was serious business most of the time. A

woman could be excused for indulging herself on occasion. And Alex Ramon was definitely an indulgence worth savoring.

Two

Alex had made a tactical error. He knew it as soon as he took Maria in his arms. Given the situation, he'd assumed that dancing was a socially acceptable convention…a polite way to pass the time.

He was wrong. Dead wrong. No matter the public venue nor the circumspect way in which he held her, nothing could erase the fact that she was soft and warm in his embrace. The slick fabric of her dress did nothing to disguise the feminine skin beneath.

He found his breath caught in his throat, lodged there by a sharp stab of hunger that caught him off guard. He'd worked so hard these past weeks that he'd let his personal needs slide. Celibacy was neither smart nor sustainable for a man his age. Certainly not when faced with such a deliciously carnal temptation.

How had he never noticed that Maria was such a tall woman...or that her cheek reached his shoulder at exactly the right spot? When he couldn't think of a good reason to let her go, one dance turned into three. Inevitably, his body responded to her nearness.

He was in heaven and hell, shuddering with arousal and unable to do a thing about it.

When Gabriel brushed past them, his petite sister in his arms, Alex remembered what he had meant to say earlier. "Maria..."

"Hmm?"

Her voice had the warm, honeyed sound of a woman pleasured by her lover. Alex cleared his throat. "You need to be careful around Gabriel Montoro."

Maria's reaction was unmistakable. She went rigid in Alex's arms and pulled away. "Excuse me?" Beautiful eyes glared at him.

He tried to continue the dance, but Maria was having none of it. So Alex soldiered on. "He's a mature, experienced man, and you're not accustomed to running in these circles. I'd hate to see him take advantage of you."

Maria went pale but for two spots of hectic color on her cheekbones. "Your concern is duly noted," she said, the words icy. "But you'll have to trust my judgment, I'm afraid. Because I don't plan to avoid him. My job is actually to get close to him, to learn his secrets, to do damage control. And I'm not a child, Alex. I'm insulted by your insinuation."

"I'm not insinuating anything," he said. "But I saw the way he looked at you."

"The man would flirt with a block of wood. I get that. But I certainly don't need you or anyone else to protect me from the big bad wolf."

"You're angry."

"Damn straight, I'm angry." Her eyes snapped with the force of her displeasure. "I was invited to be part of this delegation, and I accepted. I'm here to do a job and to do it to the best of my ability. This assignment means as much to me as it does to you. So I'll thank you to keep your advice to yourself."

"I'm sorry," he said stiffly.

Her posture erect, she gave him a stony stare. "Am I off the clock now, Mr. Ramon? May I go to my room?"

"Don't push me, Maria," he said, his teeth clenched. "It's been a long day, and the ones to come won't be much better."

She wrapped her arms around her waist in a defensive posture. "Maybe it would be best if we avoid each other when we don't have to be working together."

"If that's what you want." How had they gone from dancing to dismay so quickly?

For a brief moment he saw sadness in her gaze. His gut twisted with the sure knowledge that he had put it there.

Her bearing and her expression were dignified. "I'll see you at ten tomorrow," she said.

As he watched her walk away from him, his enjoyment in the evening went flat. He tracked her progress as she spoke to various members of the delegation and said her good-nights. The Montoros were next. Both of the Rafaels. Bella. And of course, Gabriel.

As Alex watched, Gabriel leaned down and

whispered something in Maria's ear. Whatever it was, it made her laugh.

Seeing her face light up reminded Alex of how hard she worked. In Alma, he'd never had any problem with their professional relationship. But something about Miami's heat and hedonistic ways blurred the lines between business and pleasure.

Maria was right. Part of her job was to deal with Gabriel Montoro so that he didn't embarrass his family and/or derail the plans to reinstate the monarchy.

Alex understood her priorities. But he didn't have to like them.

Maria slept poorly and woke early. Her dreams had been a jumble of Alma and Miami and Alex. Gabriel hadn't figured in those sequences at all. Which was really no surprise. Because as handsome and charismatic as the second-born Montero was, he didn't make her heart beat faster.

He amused her. He made her laugh. And she liked him a lot.

But he wasn't Alex.

After fifteen minutes of tossing and turning, it became clear she wasn't going to be able to go back to sleep. Climbing out of bed, she slipped into her swimsuit, brushed her teeth and twisted her hair into a messy knot on top of her head. This was her best chance to get in some sunbathing before the sun became blistering.

Draped from neck to midcalf in a conservative cover-up made of ecru lace, she made her way downstairs. Miami might have different standards, but Maria was a citizen of Alma and as such, subject to a certain code of dress and conduct. She would never do anything to embarrass the delegation.

Other than the occasional hotel employee, she met no one. These early-morning hours were ones she enjoyed. Filled with the promise of a new day. Peaceful.

Only when she stepped outside into the heat and humidity did things change. Not because of the weather. But because she ran headlong into a hard male body.

Catching herself and grabbing for her tote,

which threatened to spill everywhere, she looked up in consternation. "Alex."

He wore a gray T-shirt and navy running shorts. With some alarm, she realized that she had never seen his legs bare. If that weren't enough to make her gawk and stutter, she also had to take note of his broad chest and the dark patterns where sweat marked his shirt.

"Hello, Maria. You're up early."

He spoke calmly, as though their last encounter hadn't ended acrimoniously.

She nodded. "I burn easily. I thought it might be nice to spend time at the beach now. I won't be late for our meeting."

He cocked his head. "Am I such an ogre?"

The teasing glint in his eyes made her stomach clench with feelings that were definitely not professional. "Of course not."

"Good."

They both stood there waiting for the other to speak.

"You've been running," she said, as if it weren't obvious.

"Yes." When he removed his aviator sunglasses, his gaze was stormy. "It's a stress reliever."

"You have a lot on your plate."

"The Montoros aren't the only problem I'm juggling at the moment."

"What else is there?" She was genuinely curious.

"This and that." The words were flat. Without inflection. But the dark-eyed gaze held an intensity that made her nipples bead beneath two layers of fabric.

She swallowed hard. "I won't keep you then."

He took a step in her direction but stopped short. "I'd better hit the shower," he muttered. "I'm having breakfast with Rafael Montero."

"Father or son?"

"Father. He's one generation closer to the past. I'm hoping he'll help us sway the younger ones."

"He may be bitter about his own missed opportunity."

"Somehow, I doubt it. He seems to have a very casual approach to life."

"You sound as if you don't approve."

Alex shrugged, the fabric of his T-shirt clinging to a broad, muscular chest. "I'm not sure how the American personality will translate in Alma. The older people still remember days of pomp and circumstance. A laid-back monarchy may be hard to swallow."

"Are you sure we're doing the right thing?"

"No." He grimaced. "But it's the assignment we've been given. If we're in pursuit of the 'good old days,' then the monarchy is necessary for our people to feel as if life has finally returned to normal."

"Better the devil you know?"

Alex chuckled, his face lightening. "Something like that. I'd better get moving. See you at ten."

As he walked away, Maria allowed herself to track his progress. He moved with a rangy masculine gait that encompassed determination and impatience. She wondered if he ever truly relaxed.

Down on the sand, she selected a lounger and spread her towel. At this hour, the sun worshippers were few and far between. A handful of joggers. Several people walking their dogs.

She had just picked up her paperback novel when a shadow fell over her left arm. Shading her eyes with one hand, she looked up. "Gabriel. What are you doing here? I wouldn't have pegged you for an early riser."

He waited for her to move her legs to one side and then settled on the end of the chaise. "I'm not," he said, yawning. "Just now going to bed."

"Ah."

He shook his head with a wry grin. "Get your mind out of the gutter. I have a weekly poker game with some buddies."

"Did you win?"

"I always win."

Despite his reputation, she couldn't help liking the black sheep Montoro. He seemed very comfortable in his own skin, and that was a trait she admired. "Where do you live?" she asked.

"I have a condo here on the beach. But our family has a compound at Coral Gables. You should let me take you there. It's quite fabulous. You'd like it, I think…"

"I'm here to work," she said, smiling to soften the blow. "But thank you."

"If it's your stick-up-his-butt boss you're worried about, I'll invite him along, as well."

"That's not a very nice thing to say. Alex is a wonderful man. And he cares deeply about his country. I admire him very much."

"Does he know about your…devotion?"

The pause before the last word was pointed. She felt her face flush. "We're colleagues, nothing more."

"And you're okay with that?"

"I'm uncomfortable with this subject," she said, wincing inwardly at how prissy she sounded.

Gabriel waved a hand. "Fine. My apologies." He yawned again. "I need some shut-eye. Don't stay out too long and get burned, pretty Maria."

"Why are people so interested in giving me advice? I'm a grown woman, in case you haven't noticed."

Gabriel stood and stretched, his shoulders blocking out the sun. "I noticed," he said, the grin turning roguish. "But I know a lost cause when I see one. You're too nice a woman for the likes of me."

"I think I've been insulted."

"Not at all," he protested. "It's just that I don't have a great track record with sweet young things. Someone always gets a heart broken."

"Do you ever take life seriously?"

He glanced back at her as he prepared to walk away. "Not if I can help it, Maria. Not if I can help it."

* * *

An hour later she gathered her things and prepared to return to the hotel. She had just enough time to clean up and make it to Alex's suite for their meeting. They were being joined by Jean Claude, the attorney overseeing preparation of the legal documents for the restoration of the constitutional monarchy.

Maria was glad to see the lawyer for more reasons than one. He was good at what he did, but even more importantly, today he was a buffer between Alex and her. The growing awareness she had of Alex's masculinity would have to be stamped out.

For two solid hours the three of them wrangled over language and legal points. Lunch was delivered from the hotel restaurant at noon. In forty-five minutes they were at it again. From the beginning, Maria had been awestruck by the historical importance of the documents they were drafting. Now, though she still recognized the critical nature of the work, being cooped up in a small room for hours on end meant she was more than ready to call it quits when Alex finally indicated they were done.

"We can't finish everything in a day or even this week. But we've made a dent in it."

Jean Claude nodded. "When will we show the Montoros a draft?"

"Not until we have some assurance they plan to accept the offer from Alma," Alex said. "If they turn us down, we'll have to scrap everything and come up with plan B."

Maria groaned. "All this work for nothing? Please don't even hint at it. It's a dreadful thought."

Jean Claude capped his expensive pen and tucked papers into his sleek briefcase. He was in his midthirties, good-looking in a quiet, unflashy way and utterly trustworthy. Which was why he had been chosen for his current position. "I believe we must think positively. The Montoros are surely aware of their family's deep history with the country of their origin. Despite their love of the United States, blood ties will win out."

Alex ran a hand through his hair, ruffling the thick dark strands. "Let's hope you're right."

As the door closed behind Jean Claude, silence fell heavy and awkward. Maria stood, her knee bumping the leg of the table. Wincing, she picked up her things and sidled toward the exit. "Same time in the morning?" she asked, trying for a clean getaway.

Alex stopped her with nothing more than an up-raised hand. "Tomorrow is Saturday. The entire delegation has been given instructions to enjoy some time off. We'll reconvene on Monday."

Maria raised an eyebrow. "Can we afford the delay?"

"Any deadlines we come up with are artifi-cial at best. If we're to convince the Montoros of our sincerity and our pragmatism, we can't appear too desperate. It's Miami, Maria. Sun, sand, shopping."

"It's like I don't even recognize you," she teased.

The twist of his lips was self-mocking. "I do understand how to have fun, you know."

"I'll take your word for it."

Suddenly they were back to flirting again.

Alex fiddled with a stack of papers, not look-ing at her. "Did I ever tell you I had a brother? A twin?"

"No." It wasn't the kind of thing two business associates normally discussed. She wasn't going to ignore the personal overture, though. "But I'd like to hear about him…"

Alex's face was cast in shadow, the sun coming through the window at his back. Suddenly the harsh lighting made him seem a tragic figure. She shivered as if a ghost had walked over her grave.

"He died when we were ten years old," Alex said. "Complications from the flu. My parents were completely crushed."

"And what about you?"

He seemed surprised, as though no one had ever considered the grief of a sibling. "I lost a part of myself," he said slowly. "As if I'd had a limb removed. It was agony."

Maria stood frozen, her belongings clutched to her chest. "Why are you telling me this?" she asked, her voice little more than a whisper.

Alex straightened, his gaze meeting hers without hesitation. "I want us to be friends, Maria… to understand each other. You think of me as a workaholic, don't you?"

She bit her lip, evaluating her answer. "I see you as a very conscientious man."

His brooding expression touched something

deep in her heart. "I wasn't always such a stickler for the rules. But after my brother died, I felt as if I had to make up for my brother's loss by being perfect," he said. "That narrow path has become who I am now."

"A difficult way to live."

"Yes. Yes, it is." He stopped, and she saw the muscles in his throat work. "If I push too hard, call me on it. With you and Jean...with the delegation."

"It's not my place."

"It is. Because that's what I need from you."

They were separated by a space of several feet. Even so, she felt the pull of his magnetic personality. "Is that all you need?"

The words left her mouth as if someone else had spoken them. She saw his eyelashes flicker in shock and was appalled at her impulsive gaffe. "I'm sorry," she said quickly. "I shouldn't have said that."

"Do you not want to hear my answer?"

Every cell in her body trembled with uncertainty. "I think perhaps I should say no."

"I never took you for a coward, Maria."

She shook her head instinctively. "We're away

from home…in an unusual environment. We're not ourselves."

"Or maybe we're more ourselves than we're allowed to be in Alma."

His words left her breathless…literally. Until it occurred to her that she had for the moment forgotten how to breathe. Exhaling slowly, she weighed her response. Alex was an attractive, appealing man. Sharing his bed would be memorable. Of that she had no doubt.

But in the end, the two of them came from different classes. The United States might pride itself on the ability of a person with nothing to rise to the top, but Maria knew her limitations. "My mother worked in an industrial laundry ten hours a day in order to put me through school in London. And I had two jobs on top of that."

"I'm familiar with your background."

"The Ramons are aristocracy…on a par with the Montoros as far as Alma is concerned. I don't think it would be wise for you and I to do anything we might regret."

"You're throwing up barriers where none exist. The delegation was handpicked. You're here because of your skills and competence. No one looks down on you for not being a native."

"That's not what I meant and you know it."

"It's the twenty-first century, Maria."

"Maybe so. But Alma values the past. Otherwise, none of us would be here trying to reinstate the monarchy. I am proud of who I am, but I'm a realist. You and I walk different paths. Let's not forget that."

He stared at her long and hard as if he could imprint his will on her by mind control. "You asked me what I need from you."

"I shouldn't have." Her heart fluttered in her throat like a butterfly trapped.

He smiled, a totally unfair act of war. "I'll wait until you ask me again. But next time, I'll answer, Maria."

Three

She fled to her room after that, her legs spaghetti and her mouth dry. It was one thing to know she was attracted to Alex but another entirely to realize that he might be feeling the same pull.

After changing into a set of comfy knit casual wear, she pulled out her phone and initiated a FaceTime call with her mother, who was getting ready for bed. The older woman's image was clear and dear. "Hello, sweetheart. How are things going?"

"Good, Mama. I wish you could be here to see Miami. It's gorgeous."

"I'm so proud of you, Maria."

"None of this would be happening if it weren't

for all the sacrifices you've made for me." Her throat was tight suddenly.

Her mother's smile held a quiet joy. "That's a mother's job...and one I did gladly. How is Mr. Ramon?"

"Why would you ask me that?" Did her red cheeks show up on the other end?

"I'm not blind, Maria. I know you have a little crush on him."

She was too startled at her mother's perception to prevaricate. "Well, that's all there is to it. We're business associates, nothing more."

"He could do worse for a wife."

"I think you may be a tiny bit prejudiced."

They talked for five more minutes on less sensitive topics and then Maria said her good-nights. Her body was still on Alma time. The temptation to climb into bed was strong. But she knew she needed to resist if she was going to get past the jet lag.

She wasn't quite brave enough to strike out on her own in a strange city, but she had noticed a charming café in the hotel lobby as well as a series of shops with eye-catching merchandise. That would be exploration enough for one day.

Grabbing her billfold with its modest stash of American dollars, she tucked her room key and cosmetic case in a small tote and went in search of the elevator. She'd feared feeling out of place, but the hotel staff was exceptionally kind and friendly. Because she was on the early end of the dinner hour, she was escorted to a table near the window, perfectly situated to gaze out at the ocean.

After that, it was a toss-up as to whether she enjoyed the food or the view more. Though Alma supported a thriving fishing industry, the variety of seafood here in Miami was out of the ordinary. She ordered baby shrimp in a béchamel sauce with spring vegetables over angel-hair pasta. Every bite was a treat.

Afterward, she browsed the shops, trying not to let her shock show at some of the prices. Clearly the patrons of this hotel were upscale consumers with plenty of disposable income. A designer swimsuit and cover-up for twelve hundred dollars. Seventy-five-dollar rhinestone-studded beach sandals. A rattan tote that cost more that Maria earned in a month.

Fortunately, she had never needed such things

to be happy. Her mother had taught her to hunt for bargains and to stretch a euro. Though Maria admired the merchandise, it was more in the nature of appreciating exhibits at a museum. She didn't covet any of it.

When she had worked her way around the main floor of the hotel, it was still too early for bedtime. On a whim, she returned to the restaurant and decided to order dessert. Her table was not as ideally situated this go-round, but the watermelon sorbet and caramel-drizzled shortbread cookie more than made up for it.

She was sipping coffee when a familiar figure surrounded by three or four other men entered the room. Gabriel Montoro stood out no matter where she spotted him. After paying her check, she was preparing to leave when he surprised her by showing up at her table and sitting down in the empty chair.

Lifting an eyebrow, she cocked her head. "I'm on my way out. I recommend the dessert special."

Gabriel picked up an unused table knife and rotated it end over end between his fingers. "If I'd known you were eating solo, I'd have invited you to join me."

"Not necessary. Sometimes it's nice to be alone with my thoughts."

"Ouch," he said, wincing theatrically.

"Oh, for heaven's sake. I didn't mean it that way." She studied his face. For a man who claimed to live life on his own terms, she saw signs of strain. "I appreciate the thought, but I'm fine. Just trying to kill some time before I crash."

He glanced at her empty cup. "Caffeine won't help."

"So I've been told. But the coffee here is amazing."

When she stood, he did, as well. "I'll walk you to the lobby," he said.

"Aren't your friends waiting for you?"

"It's a business thing. And not that urgent."

She was unable to dissuade him. Outside the restaurant, he steered her toward a store she hadn't entered because it was mostly jewelry. "What are you doing?" she asked, frowning.

"I need your advice." He pointed toward a glass case. "Which one is the prettiest? The palm tree? Or the crab…"

She gaped. "Well, uh…" She studied the two pieces. Both were gold with delicate chains. The palm tree had a tiny diamond coconut. The crab sported two emerald eyes. "They're each beautiful."

"But?"

"Well, if I had to pick, I'd go for the crab. He's whimsical."

"Fair enough." He handed the salesclerk a platinum card.

Still baffled, Maria watched him complete the transaction. As they left the shop, Gabriel took her hand and pressed the small, lime-green bag into her palm. "This is my apology," he said. "For being a jerk yesterday. You're doing your best to help my family, and even if we don't really care, it was rude of me to say so."

Maria shoved the bag back at him, appalled. "Oh, no, Mr. Montoro. That's not necessary. Not at all. You don't owe me any apologies."

"I told you to call me Gabriel."

"Gabriel, then. It would be very inappropriate of me to accept such a valuable gift."

"Forgive me for being crass, but this is nothing. Just a way for me to soothe my conscience." He gave her a crooked smile. "I don't want you to judge my family by my behavior. I've gotta run. Sleep well, Maria."

As quickly as he had appeared, he was gone.

Maria stared at the small bag in her hand, feeling a coil of unease settle in her stomach. But what else could she have done? She couldn't afford to offend a member of the royal family.

A masculine voice, cold and clipped, interrupted her reverie. "I think I was wrong about you, Maria. I thought you were too inexperienced and naive to deal with the likes of Gabriel Montoro. But apparently you know *exactly* what you're doing."

She looked up to find Alex regarding her with disdain and patent disapproval. "This isn't what it looks like," she said.

"Cliché, my dear. Cliché. A man gives a woman he barely knows jewelry? I think I'm pretty clear about the facts."

Her temper started to simmer. "First of all, you're way out of line. Second of all, I don't have to explain myself to you. Back off, Alex. You don't know what you're talking about. Gabriel was apologizing for being antagonistic about our efforts yesterday."

"He didn't buy *me* jewelry."

"Oh, for heaven's sake. I'm going up to bed. Good night." His criticism stung, in part because she felt guilty about accepting the bauble.

She didn't make it as far as the elevator before Alex caught up with her. "I called your room, but you didn't answer," he said.

"I've been trying to stay awake a little longer. I ate dinner alone and did some window-shopping. Last time I checked, neither of those was a crime."

Alex's jaw firmed. "I'm sorry if I jumped to conclusions. I was calling to see if you wanted to walk on the beach."

The look in his dark eyes said he was telling the truth. And that his apology was sincere. Late-day stubble shadowed his jawline, giving him a rakish, dangerous air.

Her anger deflated, leaving her dangerously vulnerable to his weary charm. "I appreciate the offer, but I can barely keep my eyes open. Maybe another evening?"

He nodded. "Of course."

"Good night, Alex."

He took her wrist and then released it abruptly

when she flinched. "You've made quite an impression on the royal family," he said.

"I don't understand."

"They've invited us to spend tomorrow and Sunday at the family enclave in Coral Gables."

"The whole delegation?"

He shook his head. "Just you and me."

"Oh." Well, shoot. "I can make an excuse. It's more appropriate for you to be there."

He leaned against a marble column, legs crossed at the ankle. "I doubt that would be a popular choice, Maria. And we certainly can't take a chance on insulting them by declining. I told Mr. Montoro we'd be honored to accept. Rafael the third, that is. He seems to be receptive to our cause. Since we need all the help we can get, we're going to be there."

She sighed, feeling exhaustion wash over her. "What time?"

"Someone will pick us up at eleven in the morning. Bring everything you need for the weekend. We won't check out of our rooms, though."

"That seems extravagant, doesn't it?"

His grin was quick and surprisingly boyish.

"Relax, Maria. Your thriftiness is appreciated, but this is the big leagues."

She dreamed about that smile. And other things that left her hot and restless and agitated when she finally awoke. As she showered and dried her hair, she fretted about spending two days in a distinctly *unprofessional* atmosphere with Alex. He continued to keep her off balance. She didn't know if that was deliberate on his part or simply a function of their new circumstances.

At a quarter till eleven, she shouldered her tote and grabbed the handle of her suitcase. No point in summoning a bellman. She was leaving behind her smaller case.

In the lobby, she looked for Alex to no avail. Many people were checking out, and the sizable space was crowded. She found a corner and pulled out her phone to send a text. Before she could do so, a large hand settled on her shoulder.

"Sorry I'm late," Alex said, his expression harried. "I had to deal with a call from Alma. Some members of parliament are expecting news immediately. I tried to explain why that won't be possible."

She followed him outside. "Don't they understand that the royal family is somewhat reluctant?"

Alex donned dark sunglasses, effectively shield-
ing his gaze. "I doubt it has even occurred to
them that the Montoros may not be interested in
what we have to offer."

A uniformed chauffer held up a sign with their
names, and soon they were speeding southwest
toward Coral Gables. Maria sat back, content to
enjoy the passing view. Though Alex was dressed
casually in khaki pants and a loose ivory cotton shirt in deference to the heat, his posture remained tense as he scrolled through emails on his
phone. As deputy prime minister of commerce,
he bore an enormous workload, never more so
than now in the midst of delicate negotiations.

Maria had done her research before leaving
Alma, but at the moment all she could remember about Coral Gables was that it dated back to
the 1920s with its origin as a planned community.
And that it was home to the University of Miami.

The drive was barely half an hour on a good
day, but with traffic could be upward of forty-five
minutes. Luck was with them, and the trip was

quick. As they passed through a portion of the charming business district and turned into a residential area, Maria's jaw dropped in admiration.

Lush tropical gardens and ornate walls protected private enclaves of the wealthy and oftentimes famous. At the entrance to the Montoros' estate, the chauffeur pressed an intercom button and identified his passengers before the gate rolled back and they were granted admittance.

Even the driveway was beautiful. The ubiquitous palm trees shaded winding paths of crushed shells mixed with white sand. Feral parrots dotted the landscape with pops of intense color.

"It's like something out of a novel," Maria murmured, more to herself than to Alex.

He didn't answer, still engrossed in his work. Biting her lip, she debated how far she dared push him. "Alex."

"Hmm?" He never looked up.

"Alex." This time she put more force behind the word.

He took off his sunglasses and rubbed the heel of his hand across his forehead. "What?"

She forgave him the faint note of irritation in his voice, because she suspected he hadn't slept much last night. Between the stress and the time change, the poor man was in bad shape.

"I think you need to relax," she said. "Look around you. We're in paradise. If nothing else, we've been given an opportunity to make a good impression on the Montoros…to meet them on their turf and show that we understand them."

His chuckle was halfhearted at best. "Do we?" he asked. "Understand them, I mean? Neither you nor I have royal blood. What do we know about the obligations of rank and lineage?"

"That's true," she conceded. "But this is our chance to get beyond the obvious…to see them as they really are. Then maybe we can decide how best to cast the lure."

He put his phone away and lifted an eyebrow, gazing at her with a warm smile that curled her toes. "I'm impressed, Maria. Machiavellian machinations and intrigue. Who knew you had it in you?"

"Don't be so dramatic. All I'm saying is that we should look for their vulnerabilities…their weaknesses. We both know Alma needs the Montoros. What we need to do now is establish exactly why the Montoros need Alma. Once we've done that, the outcome should fall in our favor."

The driver pulled the limo into a circular drive-way. Before Alex could respond, Maria had gath-ered her things and stepped out of the vehicle. A uniformed housekeeper met them and ushered them inside a small guesthouse.

"Welcome," she said in softly accented English. "The Montoros are glad you are here. I have pre-pared a light meal and afterward you may want to relax for a bit. At four, someone will come to escort you to the main house to join the family."

Alex nodded. "Thank you."

The housekeeper waited patiently as they ex-plored. Maria's wide-eyed expression amused him as she took in the lavish amenities. The villa had two guest rooms, each outfitted with a massive king-size bed and expensive teak fur-nishings. The chauffeur brought in the luggage, placing Maria's in the dove-gray and shell-pink room, and Alex's in the navy-and-yellow suite.

When the tour was complete, the housekeeper held out a hand. "Would you like to eat in the sunroom?"

Alex looked at Maria and nodded. "Of course."

Soon, they were digging into a light but flavorful luncheon of fish tacos, mango salsa and conch fritters.

Alex took a sip of his really excellent pinot and shook his head. "I think they're trying to impress us."

"Isn't that our role?" Maria had devoured her food every bit as eagerly as he had.

"Maybe they want to make very clear how little they're interested in returning to Alma...in any fashion."

"Oh." Her crestfallen look urged him to comfort her. But the unexpected wave of tenderness made him uneasy. She caused him to feel things that were inappropriate at best and dangerously seductive at worst. How could he fulfill his mission if he were constantly derailed by his baser instincts?

A life of public service meant subverting his own needs for the greater good. For the benefit of his country and for the sake of his pride he would have to ignore the way she made him feel.

She had left her blond hair loose today, confined only by two small tortoiseshell clips, one at either temple. Though he knew she came from a background far less privileged than his, she carried herself with a regal grace and dignity that surpassed her years.

He had suggested her as one of the team for this trip, but ultimately, she had been chosen by the committee. Her talent and hard work impressed everyone who witnessed her in action.

She'd been right to call him on his preoccupation. *Nothing* at the moment was more important than the Montoros.

As they finished their meal, the housekeeper hovered, spiriting away empty plates and keeping their glasses full. At last, she left them alone.

Alex cleared his throat. "Would you like a nap?"

"The answer is yes, but I'm not going to take one. I'm determined to beat this jet lag. How about a walk instead?"

"You do know it's hot as hell out there."

She wrinkled her nose. "Yes. But it's Florida. I've never been here."

He held out his hands. "Far be it from me to stop you. I'll tag along to make sure you don't get lost."

Maria changed clothes so quickly he was stunned. Instead of the subdued navy dress she had worn earlier, she came out of her room wearing white shorts that showcased her long, tanned legs and a raspberry-colored tank top. Her hair was now caught up in a free-falling ponytail. The outfit shaved half a dozen years off her age, reminding him again of how young she was.

He swallowed against a tight throat. "That was fast."

She shrugged. "My mother believes in a woman being herself. Too many lotions and potions breed vanity…or so she claims. I started sneaking mascara and lip gloss when I was fourteen."

"Such a rebel," he teased.

"I tried to behave. I really did, because I adored my mother, even as a bratty teenager. But I wanted to be like all the other girls."

"Not such a terrible failing."

"I suppose not. But she came home from work early one day before I'd had a chance to wash my face, and she was so…"

"Angry?"

"No. Not that. It was worse. I had disappointed her. She told me that it was a mistake for a girl to primp and paint herself to attract a boy. That I should be proud of who I was inside. That the exterior didn't matter."

"Wise words."

"Yes. But they came from a place of pain. I never knew the details, though it was no secret that my father abandoned her before I was born. When it came to love, she had chosen poorly, and she paid for it the rest of her life. My goal has been to earn enough money to set her up in a little retirement flat. I owe her so much. And I want to give her a chance to enjoy life while she is still strong and healthy."

"You're a good daughter."

For a fleeting second he witnessed a surprising vulnerability in her aquamarine eyes. "I hope so."

Four

As they exited the small house, Alex pondered Maria's words. He knew she was ambitious. Unlike some people, he didn't see that as a negative in a woman. He'd like to think he was more of an enlightened male than some of his contemporaries.

But what if Maria's ambitions had more to do with securing a future for her mother and herself than for simply rising in the ranks of government service? Did she want a husband and children? Or had her mother's experience made Maria reluctant to entrust a man with her future? The more he thought about it, the less he was sure of anything.

What bothered him the most was the faint but insistent notion that she might be setting herself up to land in a Montoro's bed. Gabriel's to be exact. Did Maria have fantasies of becoming a princess?

Almost instantly, Alex was ashamed of his doubts. He had no basis at all for such a supposition. Merely his own jealousy. Though he knew a relationship with Maria was not likely to be good for either of them, he winced at the thought of her being with another man. Surely it was a dog-in-the-manger attitude.

As they wandered the grounds, he tried to keep his mind on the flora and fauna and not on the long-legged grace of the beauty in front of him. The more time he spent in Maria's company, the less control he had over his fantasy life. Already, he'd been awakened twice on this trip by intensely erotic dreams.

Now, with her three feet ahead, his hands itched to feel the silky hair that tumbled down her back. It bounced and swung as she walked. In his imagination he could see that same hair spread out across his pillow, those wide-set eyes, drowsy with passion, staring up at him.

Damn it. He was hard and hot and horny, none of which were appropriate conditions for the man who was supposed to be orchestrating a diplomatic dance that could affect thousands of lives.

Clenching his jaw, he concentrated on naming the flowering shrubs they passed. Anything to keep from staring at a heart-shaped butt and narrow waist made for the grasp of a man's hands.

Despite her claim of jet lag, Maria seemed indefatigable. The various pathways were clearly marked, so it was easy to circle back around in the direction of their accommodations. At the very last turn, they lingered beside a small lagoon, taking advantage of a patch of shade.

A pair of peacocks strutted on the far bank. Birdsong echoed from every direction. Maria leaned against a tree trunk, propping one foot behind her. "I like the wildness," she said, smiling dreamily. "The landscape is passionate and alive."

"If it were you, would you go back to a country where you had never lived? Simply to fulfill a destiny you didn't choose?"

She gazed toward the water, her profile as familiar to him now as his own face in the mirror.

"I honestly don't know. My life is so different. Once my mother is gone, I'll never have a chance to press the issue of my father's identity. And she won't even discuss her own family, because they threw her out when she ended up pregnant and unmarried. So the idea of having a family tree that can be traced back almost two thousand years is hard for me to grasp. My past is a blank slate."

"I'm sorry," he said.

"It is what it is."

She wasn't trying to elicit his sympathy. Her words were matter-of-fact. He wondered, though, if she recognized the vein of wistful sadness he heard in them.

Her skin glowed with heat and perspiration. It occurred to him in that quiet moment that her beauty was intrinsic, not dependent at all on the paints and potions she had so whimsically described. She might look much like this after a bout of energetic lovemaking.

Shifting restlessly from one foot to the other, he fought the urge to take her in his arms. Clearing his throat, he glanced at his watch. "We should get back and clean up."

She nodded, smiling at him with such sweet openness that his heart clenched in his chest. "I'm glad I was able to come on this trip. I know you put in a good word for me, and I'm grateful."

He stared at her, his body rigid with desire. "I don't want your gratitude, Maria."

Hurt flickered in her eyes, only to be replaced by dawning surprise as she realized what he wasn't saying. "I asked you before what you needed from me. And you wouldn't answer."

"Correction. I *didn't* answer because you weren't willing to listen."

She straightened from her relaxed pose against the tree and took a step in his direction. "And if I'm ready now?"

He shuddered, no longer able to hide the hunger that rode him hard. "Come here," he said, tugging her by the hand until she landed against his chest. He linked his hands at the small of her back, allowing himself one tiny nibble of a shell-like ear.

She looked up at him, her eyes huge. "Men are strange creatures."

He choked out a laugh. "What does that mean?"

"I'm all sweaty and icky."

Inhaling sharply, he shook his head. "Definitely not icky. Trust me on that one." He found her mouth with his, going in for a quick pass and then lingering to taste every nuance of warm, willing woman.

Maria was not shy, but there was a certain hesitance in her response, a tiny awkwardness that perhaps signified a lack of experience. That same pesky tenderness surfaced, making him want to protect her from himself. And wasn't that a conundrum...

Finally, her arms went around his neck. Now they were pressed chest-to-chest, hip-to-hip. There was no way she could miss the state of his body. He was hard everywhere.

Though it took everything he had, he kept the kiss gentle, the embrace circumspect. They were standing where anyone could see them. And they had a very critical appointment in less than an hour.

One more minute. That's all he needed. His tongue stroked hers. "Hell, Maria. You make me forget my name."

"Alex," she whispered, straining against him, standing on tiptoe. "Smart, sexy, adorable Alex."

"Adorable?" He frowned, trying to focus as she sucked on his bottom lip.

"Adorable," she said firmly. "You're so serious and dedicated and straight-arrow. It's lovable and charming."

He forced himself to release her, though when she clung to him in protest, his resolve weakened. His heart slamming in his chest like a pile driver, he took her wrists in his hands and dragged them away from his neck. "I'm not feeling at all dedicated right now, Maria. If it weren't for the possibility of alligators in that lagoon, I'd be tempted to pull you down on the ground and have my adorable wicked way with you."

"Alligators?" Her shriek sent a flock of birds skyward.

If he'd hoped to derail the possibility of sex, he'd succeeded beyond his wildest dreams. His companion looked scared to death.

He shook his head in bemusement. "You do know where we are, right? Alligator alley?"

"I didn't think they were everywhere." She clung to his arm as he led her back toward their quarters.

Alex ushered her inside the villa and shut the

door. "I didn't mean to frighten you. Gators aren't aggressive as a rule. Though they might grab the occasional cat or dog."

"Oh, Lord." When she went white, he realized his assurances weren't helping.

"Go take your shower," he said. "As long as you stay out of unknown pools and ponds, you've got nothing to worry about, I swear." He leaned down for one last kiss. "I'll protect you."

Maria turned the water as hot as she could bear it, stepping into the shower and trying to stop shaking. Maybe her fear was irrational, but while she could handle the occasional mouse or nasty spider, alligators were beyond her experience. Maybe this was what people meant when they said every Eden has its serpent.

Miami and Coral Gables were beautiful beyond belief. Lush...tropical...a garden paradise. She'd never anticipated a dark side.

As she dried off and re-dressed in the outfit she'd worn earlier, she hoped she had chosen appropriate attire for the weekend. Unfortunately, there was no manual for how to hobnob with royalty in America.

Her navy linen sheath dress was very plain, its only adornment a trio of quirky wooden buttons on either shoulder. Her shoes were low-heeled strappy sandals in a neutral shade with cork soles. She stared in the mirror. Too casual? Not casual enough?

The decision was moot now, because she didn't have enough clothing with her for endless choices. Truthfully, it probably didn't matter. She was not a key player in this drama. Alex was the one in the hot seat. The Montoros would be grilling him, not Maria. Poor Alex.

She finished drying her hair and brushed it out, leaving it as it had been when she arrived. The clips kept it off her face. Presumably this afternoon's gathering would be inside an air-conditioned space. One thing she had already learned about Florida was that even if the outside temperatures were sweltering, inside most buildings, it was cold enough to hang meat.

Alex was waiting in the living room when she went in search of him. His smile was automatic and held no hint that only minutes earlier they had been passionately entwined in a kiss that had made her weak with longing.

She decided to match his air of calm. "Are we ready?"

He nodded. At that same moment the doorbell chimed. A young man, probably Maria's age, stood waiting with a polite posture. His grin was quick and easy. A navy knit polo shirt, stretched across his broad shoulders, identified him as an employee of Montoro Enterprises.

"I'm here to take you to the main house," he said. "The Jeep's right outside."

The vehicle was spotless, though perhaps not designed for women wearing dresses. Maria's cheeks flamed when she was forced to accept Alex's help climbing into the rear seat. The two men sat up front.

It dawned on her that this compound must be even larger than she had imagined, because it took five minutes to drive to their destination. All the buildings, large or small, had been designed in the same vein, with whitewashed stucco walls and blue tile roofs.

Most of the places they passed she couldn't identify, but she did see a gardening shed and a transportation corral that housed multiple golf carts. When they arrived at the Montoros' residence, she was not surprised to find that it was the largest building on the property.

It was a work of art...two stories, with wrap-around porches, ceiling fans and rattan furnishings. And there were windows...lots of windows. The glass was probably tinted, because otherwise, the sun would bake the inhabitants.

Their escort parked at the base of a shallow set of steps and abandoned them. "Just knock," he said, whistling as he wandered away.

Maria looked at Alex askance. "I guess we're on our own."

He shaded his eyes and looked around with curiosity. "I guess we are." He didn't seem a fraction as nervous as she felt. But then again, his family was every bit as prestigious as the Montoros, though not royal. If Alex so desired, he could probably be elected to lead the country when the current prime minister's term was over.

Together, she and Alex ascended the stairs. Moments after Alex rang the buzzer, a honey-skinned gray-haired man answered the door. He was dressed much like Alex in clothes that gave deference to the climate, though his manner was anything but relaxed. An English butler couldn't have been more dignified.

"Welcome to Casa Montoro," he said. "The family awaits you in the salon."

The house reminded Maria of a spread she'd once envied in *Architectural Digest*. Every detail was harmonious perfection. Polished hardwood floors, colorful rag rugs. And views. Wow. One entire wall of glass framed the ocean in the distance.

When she and Alex entered the large room, Rafael III jumped to his feet. "You're here at last. We're honored to welcome you to our home." He shook Alex's hand and kissed Maria on both cheeks.

One glance around the assemblage told Maria that the key players in this drama were present. Rafael's three children—Gabriel, Bella and Rafael IV. Juan Carlos II, the cousin. And, last but not least, the frail but indomitable Isabella Salazar.

At seventy-three, she should still have a number of good years ahead of her, but her body had been ravaged with Parkinson's. Though bound to a wheelchair when she was able to get out of bed, she was an imposing figure. Grandmother to Juan Carlos and great-aunt to his cousins, Isabella wielded considerable influence. *And* she was a proponent of the old ways. Which made her automatically an ally.

With the exception of Isabella, Maria and Alex had met everyone the night of the reception. Knowing that, and as a matter of courtesy, Rafael took them immediately to sit with his aunt.

The old woman might have been trapped in a broken body, but her mind was sharp and her eyesight keen. "Do you know why we invited the two of you today?" she asked, the words abrupt.

Maria gulped inwardly and saw by Alex's reaction that he was as taken aback as she was. Alex recovered first. "Not exactly, ma'am."

"You're wondering why we didn't bring the entire delegation out here."

Alex was brave enough to give her the truth. "The thought crossed our minds."

"It's simple, boy. Your people are supposed to have the weekend free to relax and enjoy Miami. Correct?"

"Yes."

"So we left them alone. But the two of you

are here because Gabriel over there owned up to being a bit of an ass when he first met you. He's hotheaded, but he's a good boy, and he thought better of his actions. On behalf of our extended family, we want to apologize for any ill manners on the part of the Montoros, and I assure you, you'll find us receptive to your proposal when it is ready."

Maria glanced around the room, not at all convinced. Gabriel and Bella wore identical mulish expressions. Rafael, the father, was sober. Rafael, the son, appeared uncomfortable. Only Juan Carlos, who was not a key player in all of this, seemed calm.

Alex, ever the politician, spoke carefully. "Maria and I are very appreciative of the invitation to be here with you today. But apologies are unnecessary. This is a difficult time for everyone involved. I'd expect there to be certain tensions along the way. Hopefully, in the end we'll be able to work out solutions beneficial to Alma and to your family, as well."

Rafael III nodded. He had allowed his aunt the courtesy of speaking due to her age and position, but now he took control. "Mr. Ramon, my elder son and I would like to sit down with you in my office and go over our business situation so you have a clear idea of our responsibilities. I've asked Bella and Gabriel to entertain Ms. Ferro."

Juan Carlos, the tall young man with the reserved manner, spoke up. "My grandmother has a social engagement this afternoon, and I have promised to escort her. But we will rejoin you for dinner later this evening. Please excuse us."

When those two left the room, Maria saw Alex glance at Gabriel with an inscrutable expression. Was he unhappy that Maria was to spend time with the Montoro bad boy...even with Bella as chaperone? If he was, it was too bad. Maria couldn't refuse without insulting her hosts, and besides, she didn't want to refuse. Gabriel was an interesting man whose company she enjoyed, and this would also be an opportune moment to get acquainted with the very young and very pretty Bella.

As Rafael escorted his son and Alex out a door on the opposite side of the salon, Bella clapped her hands softly. "Alone at last. I'm so tired of all this Alma talk. No offense, Miss Ferro."

"None taken. But please call me Maria."

Gabriel squeezed his sibling's shoulders. "My baby sister thought you might enjoy the pool. She has enough bikinis to outfit every woman in a twenty-mile radius. But if you're not a sun worshipper, Maria, we can go out on the boat instead."

"The pool sounds delightful, actually. And I did bring a suit. As long as you have sunscreen, I'd love a swim."

Bella wrinkled her nose. "I'll let you two be energetic. I had a late night last night, so I may snooze behind my sunglasses."

Gabriel chuckled. "Maria, it's no secret that my Bella is a party girl. She knows every hot spot in Miami. But somehow she manages to stay out of trouble."

"Which is more than *you* ever did at my age," Bella shot back with a fond smile that told Maria these two were close, indeed.

Seeing Bella in a bikini made Maria very glad she had brought her own swimsuit. The younger woman's style and body were flawless. Maria had a decent self-image, but she was more than happy to don the conservative navy maillot she'd brought along.

When she and Bella exited the changing cabana, Gabriel was already in the pool, his broad shoulders gleaming wet and golden in the blistering sun. The man was incredibly handsome, but oddly, he didn't increase her heart rate one bit. Apparently she had a thing for focused, über-conscientious oil barons with black hair and deep brown eyes.

Determined to forget about work and Alex and Alma for a while, she stepped up onto the diving board, walked to the end and executed a simple dive into the aquamarine water.

Five

When she surfaced, she laughed out loud, exhilarated by the feel of the silky cool water against her overheated skin. "This is amazing," she said. "It was raining when we left home...in fact, it had been raining for a week. I could get used to perpetual sunshine."

Bella adjusted the back of her lounge chair and smoothed her beach towel before stretching out with an audible sigh. "Perfection gets boring after a while, Maria. Ask our older brother."

Gabriel slicked a hand through his hair, sending droplets of water flying, his green eyes gleaming. "You're not being fair to Rafe, Bella. You try being CEO of Montoro Enterprises and see how you like it."

Bella donned dark glasses, shuddering. "No thank you. My job is to spend money, not make it."

When his sister subsided in a somnolent pose, Gabriel swam to where Maria paddled lazily in the deep end. "She's putting on a show for you," he said in a low whisper. "Bella gets tagged as flighty and shallow, but my sister is a good actress. Few outside the family know about her charity work and her passion for preserving the environment."

"Why the charade?"

"I think people made assumptions about her as a teenager, and at that vulnerable age, the criticism hurt. Now she goes out of her way to appear as a wealthy diva without a care in the world."

"How does she feel about the possibility of becoming a royal and living in Alma?"

He shrugged. "I don't really know. I'm the only one who has been clear from the beginning about my feelings. The rest of them are playing their cards close to the chest. Maybe Bella likes the idea of starting over somewhere new, who knows? But we're still being premature…right?"

Maria sighed. "What's so terrible about re-claiming a throne and a legacy that are your birthright? The history of the Montoro family is inextricably interwoven with Alma's past."

"You're talking about tearing my family apart. If Rafe agrees to this madness, he'll move across the ocean."

"You've heard of jets, haven't you?"

Gabriel flicked water at her. "It's not the same. My family is exceedingly close. If we agree to accept this offer from Alma, someone will have to stay here to run the business. Decades of work have gone into making our company a player on two continents."

"I don't know what to tell you, Gabriel. This proposal from Alma to your family has taken on a life of its own. I sympathize with your position, but I have to move ahead with my responsibilities until someone tells me differently."

"You think our family is going to accept, don't you?"

She weighed her answer. "I hope so. Alma has suffered through years of deprivation and corruption and abuse. Now, finally, good things are beginning to happen. Having a Montoro on the throne again would be a huge boost to morale and for the identity of the people. Can you blame me for wanting to see that come to pass?"

For once, there wasn't a hint of humor or teasing on his face. "No. I suppose not."

"Let's wait and see what happens. A lot of the outcome hinges on your brother. It's a shame your father isn't eligible to ascend the throne, though. He's a very young fifty, and so exuberant and gregarious. I think he would have made an impressive king."

"My brother will, as well…if it comes to that."

"You're very protective of your family, aren't you? And very proud."

"Any one of them is worth three dozen of me. I'm a cynic, Maria…and I don't trust easily. This whole monarchy thing stinks of self-serving on the part of your chosen country. It's insulting for my family to be trotted out as puppet royalty so the merchants of Alma can sell postcards and T-shirts."

She studied his Greek god features, seeing the restless agitation and his genuine dismay. "Give us a chance," she said quietly. "I think you'll be pleasantly surprised when you see the actual proposal. No one wants to diminish the stature of the Montoros. In fact, quite the opposite. You have royal blood. That means something."

His expression lightened, but she sensed he wasn't convinced. They both clung to opposite sides of the ladder, their legs moving lazily in deep water. For a brief moment, she considered the odd situation. Perhaps this was the equivalent of doing business on the golf course.

Although Gabriel was a big flirt, he had neither said nor done anything to make her feel uncomfortable at being so close to him and wearing such skimpy clothing. They had spoken of deep, important matters. If anything, being in the water had kept their conversation from overheating.

It was difficult to fly off the handle when in the midst of such sybaritic surroundings. Truthfully, she felt sorry for Gabriel. It must be difficult to see the people he loved struggling with such gargantuan changes.

"You'll be royalty, too," she said quietly. "If this plays out like I think it will."

"No way," he said firmly. "If my brother decides he has to fall on the sword, I'll support him in every way I know how. But I'm not going to be a damned royal. Bella tried to make me play Prince Eric to her Ariel doll when we were little kids. I didn't like it then, and I haven't changed in that regard. I know who I am and who I'm not."

She didn't waste her breath explaining the role he would play in his brother's coronation…or in describing the richly ornamental robes and jewels of state that had been hidden away for decades. Time enough for him to get used to all that later. Right now, she had two jobs. One—impress upon him the importance of the Montoros to Alma's rebirth. And two—determine what, if any, of his bad-boy past might pop up and cause damage to the royal family's reputation.

"You can fight it all you want," she said earnestly, "but blood will tell, as they say."

"You're wrong," he said firmly. "If I were to cut your arm or you mine, our blood would look the same. I'm an American. We built this country on principles of equality."

"That may be so, but you can't rewrite history." Bella lifted her head, sliding her sunglasses to the top of her head to glare at them. "Oh, for God's sake. Give it a rest. Can't we talk about books or movies or baseball? The two of you are giving me a headache."

Gabriel touched Maria's shoulder briefly. "Though I hate to admit it, my sister is right. This is a day for relaxing."

Alex stepped outside just in time to see Gabriel caress Maria's bare arm. The surge of primitive fury that racked him found no outlet. He was forced to clench his jaw and walk forward as if nothing was wrong.

Maria's face lit up when she saw him, appeasing his displeasure somewhat. "Alex…did you bring something to change into?"

Gabriel shaded his eyes. "Plenty of swim trunks in the cabana."

Alex debated his options. What he would *like* to do was spirit Maria back to their villa and make love to her until the sun came up. But since that wasn't an option, he might as well make the best of things.

By the time he had stripped down, changed and made it back to the pool, his feet were uncomfortably warm from the hot concrete. Even Bella had given up on sunbathing and was now frolicking in the water. Someone had set up a net midway across the pool, and brother and sister had apparently formed a team.

Maria beckoned him. "Hurry. They think they're champions, but I told them you were a big athlete at university."

"Not in volleyball," he said mildly, sliding into the cool water with an inward sigh of bliss.

"Doesn't matter," Maria declared. "I think we can take them."

Maria's scantily clad body was a definite handicap to his concentration. But when Gabriel scored two points right off the bat, Alex dragged his attention from her rounded breasts and sexy wet hair to the competition at hand. With Maria gazing at him in supplication, he brought his A game. The adrenaline rush of competition was a great stress reliever. And it was damn fun.

Maria and Bella were both nimble and coordinated. They set up shots and the two men took turns smashing points over the net. Time and again Maria dove for saves, her face dripping water and her eyes lit up with laughter.

He was, at some level, struck dumb by her beauty. She was so alive, so eager, so joyful. He felt the pull in his gut and wanted badly to kiss her. Because of Alex's addled state, Gabriel was able to spike the ball for yet another point. The smug smile on the other man's face told Alex that his opponent might have put Maria on Alex's team on purpose.

Of course, watching her across the net with Gabriel would have been just as bad.

After each team won two games apiece, it was mutually decided to play best three out of five. All four competitors were out of breath from battling the water to reach the ball.

Alex shot Maria a glance, trying not to notice the way her nipples beaded against the thin fabric of her suit. "You okay?"

"Of course." She moved closer and lowered her voice. "And I want to win."

He grinned, for the moment forgetting his responsibilities and his governmental role. "Then let's do it."

The game was fierce and quick, each side battling for supremacy. The Montoro team edged ahead by two or three only to be matched by Alex and Maria in the next few minutes.

Bella was short, but she was a master at setting up the ball. It was clear that she and her brother had teamed up before. Maria was taller and could occasionally punch a shot over the net, but mostly she fed the ball to Alex.

They had made it to game point a half-dozen times when the older Rafael appeared poolside and signaled their attention with a broad smile. "Dinner in half an hour. Don't make me come after you."

Alex grinned at his partner. Her cheeks were pink from the sun or from exertion or both. Her eyes sparkled amid spiky lashes. "We've come too far to lose," he said.

"My feelings exactly."

In that moment, he knew that they could have as easily been talking about their mission as the game.

Alex turned back to the net. "We're ready."

Bella pumped a perfect serve deep into her opponent's watery court. Maria fielded it, set it up for Alex, and he shot it over the net. Back and forth, back and forth.

Finally, Maria began to tire. But she still made her play and got the ball to Alex. He jumped, ready to spike a point, when he lost his balance and fell into the net. Gabriel seized the moment and hammered the ball into enemy territory.

Unfortunately, the driving slam struck Maria in the face, and down she went.

"Good God." Alex's heart stopped. Vaguely he was aware of shouts from Bella and Gabriel, but he got to Maria first and dragged her up out of the water. Her eyes were closed, her face contorted in pain. Already a large knot had formed over her left eye.

Gabriel shoved his way close. "Let me see her."

Alex glared at him. "You could have knocked her out."

Gabriel touched her hair. "Damn, I'm sorry. Stupid competitive urges. I should be shot."

Maria tried to stand up. "I'm fine. No permanent damage."

Alex tightened his arms around her. "Don't move. I've got you." He strode toward the ladder, Gabriel at his elbow. Gabriel nudged him. "Give her to me and hop out. I'll hand her up to you."

Alex bristled. "No. I can handle this." Awkwardly, he tried to reach the first step.

Bella got between him and the ladder, her expression combative. "You two boneheads are acting like Neanderthals. Back off. Maria can get up the ladder on her own." She bit her lip. "Can't you, honey?"

Maria nodded. "Of course."

Reluctantly, Alex allowed Maria to wriggle out of his embrace. He steadied her when she was on her feet. "Are you sure?"

"Yes." Her face was pale, but she managed the three steps and made it up onto the side of the pool.

Alex sprinted behind her and picked her up again.

Gabriel and Bella followed him. "There's a sofa in the cabana," Bella said.

As Alex deposited his precious cargo on the comfy couch, Gabriel frowned. "I'll call 9-1-1."

"No, no, no." Maria sat up despite their protests. "It's a bump on the head. That's all. Give me some aspirin and I'll be fine."

Maria was embarrassed and mortified. Her three companions hovered like broody hens. And despite her wishes, the Montoros' private physician was summoned. The speed at which he arrived startled her.

Everyone was sent out of the cabana while the doctor did his exam. He was kind and gentle and thorough. At last he gave her the all clear. No concussion, but plenty of headaches on the way.

When the other three were allowed to return, Maria struggled to sit up. "We have to change. Dinner is already late because of me."

Gabriel crouched beside her. "Let Alex take you back to the villa. You're in no shape to suffer through a formal meal. My family will understand, of course. If you feel better in the morning, you're welcome to join us for breakfast."

Bella nodded. "My bull-in-the-china-shop brother is right. I'll have dinner sent down to you. Take the evening to recover." She gathered up Maria's things, as well as Alex's, and tucked them in a large canvas tote.

Gabriel handed Alex a set of keys. "Take the golf cart that's outside. Call the main house if you need anything or if she gets worse."

"I'm sitting right here," Maria said, exasperated. What was it about powerful men that made them feel as if they had to control the world?

Alex steadied her as she stood. "Take it slow."

Outside, Bella gave her a hug. "I'm so sorry about this."

Gabriel said nothing, his expression frustrated and guilty.

"It's nothing," Maria insisted. "I'll be fine."

At last she and Alex were allowed to escape. He drove the cart expertly, of course. And though she couldn't remember for sure where all the turns were, Alex tracked the route without error.

Back at their lodging, she held him off with an upraised hand. "I can walk inside." Still wearing a damp swimsuit, she felt distinctly at a disadvantage, even though Alex was half-naked, as well. Perhaps *because* Alex was half-naked. Despite her pounding headache, she wasn't immune to his overt masculinity.

She was accustomed to seeing him dressed to the nines, sartorial perfection from head to toe. And *that* man was wildly attractive.

But something about all the bare skin between them sent a pulse thrumming low in her belly. Alex's lightly hair dusted chest and powerful thighs said louder than words that he was a virile man in his prime. If she hadn't been indisposed, she'd have been hard-pressed not to jump his bones. As it was, she had to admire him with a modicum of restraint.

Though she would die before admitting it, she was woozy by the time they made it inside and to her room. Alex allowed her to move at her own pace, but he stayed close. At last, she faced him with a wry smile. "I'm going to take a shower. I'll be careful, I promise."

"Is that wise?" She could see that he didn't like her choice. But short of tying her to a chair, he had no recourse but to step back and close the bedroom door.

When he was gone, her legs gave out and she sat down on the side of the bed. Her head hurt like crazy. When she chanced a peek in the mirror over the dresser, she groaned. Her eye and part of her cheek were swollen, giving her face an odd, lopsided look.

Well, if she'd ever had any hope of luring Alex into her bed, all bets were off. He might be willing to kiss hot-and-sweaty Maria, but what guy would be attracted to a woman who looked like she'd gone three rounds with a boxing champ?

Dispirited and hurting, she gathered her clean

undies and her short gown and robe. Their deep plum color should have boosted her spirits, but all she could think about was how her eye was probably going to be a perfect match.

It actually hurt for the water in the shower to hit her face, so she turned the faucet away and managed to wash the chlorine out of her hair without too much discomfort. After drying off and donning her sleepwear, she sat and dried her hair.

There were times—now being one of them—that she debated cutting her hair. Its length was pure vanity. But the thought of chopping it off made her wince. So she put up with the time it took to wash and dry it.

When she was done, her aches and pains had begun to make themselves felt in earnest. The doctor had left some painkillers. But she needed to take them with food. And, besides, she was starving.

Barefoot, she padded into the living room. Her robe was thigh length, but perfectly respectable, especially given the climate. She found Alex sprawled on the sofa, flipping channels. He was dressed in the casual shirt and slacks he had worn on arrival.

He jumped to his feet. "The food's in the kitchen. Are you interested in eating?"

She nodded, a lump in her throat. The genuine concern on his face and in his dark eyes made her feel cared for and protected. It was a warm, fuzzy sensation. "I'm really hungry," she said softly.

He insisted on seating her at the table and serving her plate from the variety of dishes on the counter.

Maria was barely conscious of what she ate. The food was hot and delicious, but she tasted little of it. She was far too aware of the tension in the room. She remembered their kiss earlier in the day, and it was a good bet Alex did, too.

Six

Alex tried not to let Maria see how worried he was about her. Fatigue was visible in the curve of her shoulders and the pale cast of her skin. She seemed to be holding herself upright by sheer stubbornness.

The knot where the volleyball had made contact with her eye socket had already gone down some, but the bruise was blooming rapidly.

He joined her at the table to eat, though he had no real interest in food. "I was going to offer you a glass of wine," he said. "But I thought better of it. Didn't seem like a good idea if you're taking pain pills."

She pulled a prescription bottle from the pocket

of her robe. "The doctor said I can take two at a time, but I'm going to start with one and see how I do."

As he watched, she shook one tablet into her hand and washed it down with water. When her head tilted back, the silky fabric of her nightwear shifted and pulled, making it clear that she was bare underneath. Which made perfect sense, of course. But it also played havoc with his physical state.

He cleared his throat. "It's not late, but you may want to go on to bed."

She shook her head. "I've only now adjusted to the time change. I don't want to start over again. Do you think we could watch a movie?"

He would have done anything she asked in that moment. "Of course," he said, the words gruff.

When they finished their meal, he gathered the dishes and put them in the sink. Maria sat staring at him. "This is weird," she said.

He turned to look at her. "What do you mean?"

"We have a working relationship. And a very important job to do. But suddenly you're having to play nurse. I'm sorry."

He couldn't help himself. Wiping his hands on

a dry cloth, he went to her and gathered her hair gently, tucking it over her shoulder so it covered one breast. "Nothing is weird unless we let it be. I kissed you today, Maria. And you kissed me back. Your bump on the head is unfortunate, but I don't regret this time together."

Taking her hand in his, he slowly pulled her to her feet.

When he scooped her into his arms, she protested as she had earlier. "I can walk into the living room."

His arms tightened a fraction. He was a bit drunk on the smell and feel of her. "Humor me. I happen to like having you in my arms."

When he set her gently on the sofa, she stared up at him, wide-eyed. "Are you sure about this?"

She wasn't referring to the movie, of course. "I'm not sure about anything here in Florida," he joked. "Least of all this. But I plan to go with the flow."

He felt her gaze boring into his back as he selected a disc and inserted it into the Blu-ray player and muted the volume. The movie didn't really matter. He had other plans.

When he joined her, she wrapped her arms

around her waist and tugged at the hem of her robe. "I've known you for a very long time, Alex...and even on your wildest days, I'd never call you a go-with-the-flow kind of guy."

Her lips quirked, her teasing smile softening what might have been a criticism. But the gentle light in her eyes told him she understood what he was saying.

An attack of conscience struck him as he settled into the soft, plump couch cushions. "If you'd rather watch this alone, I'll leave you. I've plenty of work to do in my room."

One small hand landed on his thigh...not moving...just searing him with heat. "I want you to stay."

He swallowed, for one brief second questioning his sanity. There was a better than even chance that Gabriel Montoro had plans for Maria. Could Alex risk offending a member of the royal family in the midst of delicate negotiations?

But when his hand closed over Maria's, their fingers twining together, he sucked in a deep breath as he realized that for once in his life he was prepared to put his personal wishes and feelings before his obligations.

Gently, giving her every chance to protest, he scooped her into his lap. Her head settled against his collarbone as if he had been holding her like this for a lifetime. "How do you feel?" he asked.

She stroked his jaw with a single finger. "Well enough for whatever you have in mind."

"I seriously doubt that." If she knew what he was thinking, what he wanted, she might run for the hills. "We'll take this slow," he promised. "Tonight and always. I don't want to hurt you."

"I'm a grown woman, Alex. You may have a lot of responsibilities, but I'm not one of them."

The spark of temper reminded him that his Maria was a female of strength and purpose. "I can't apologize for wanting to take care of you. You bring out the gentleman in me."

She curled a hand behind his neck, dragging his head lower to press her lips to his. "Maybe I don't want the gentleman," she muttered. "Kiss me, Alex."

Whatever measure of control he'd maintained up until that second finally snapped. Easing her down onto her back, he parted the lapels of her robe. Lust was a kick to his chest. But it was wrapped in wonder and tenderness. He touched a tight, rosy nipple. "You're so damned beautiful." The words stuck in his throat. He felt he could barely breathe.

"I look like a clown."

He heard the feminine pique in her words and had to smile. "You may be a trifle the worse for wear, dear Maria, but it only makes me want you more."

She rolled her eyes at him. "Is that how you win over your conquests? With outright lies?"

He put his hand, palm flat over her heart, cupping the curves of her breast. "I work too hard to have much of a personal life," he said, willing to be brutally honest if it meant relieving her misgivings. "And when I do spend time with a woman, I am always honest."

"Somehow, I believe you." Her chest rose and fell with her quickened breathing. Despite her poor face, all he could see was the arousal darkening her gaze.

The sofa was oversize and perfectly designed for the things he had in mind. Easing down beside her on one elbow, he separated the robe completely, taking in the minuscule pair of satiny black undies she wore. He traced the tiny elastic edging, feeling the soft skin of her flat stomach.

Reluctantly, he gave her the truth he had promised. "We're not going to be reckless, Maria. I draw the line at making love to an injured woman."

"That's not fair. I get a vote, don't I?"

He shook his head. "Not tonight." Though it would cost him dearly, he decided he could play with fire. Moving carefully so as not to cause her any distress, he sucked in a sharp breath when touching her hardened his sex to the point of pain. "God, you make me crazy," he groaned.

Kissing her was like diving into a pool of quicksand. But aligning their bodies so that warm, feminine flesh nestled against him was far worse. Shaking, he slid a hand between her legs, noting the warmth and dampness that told him she was ready for his possession.

The foreplay tormented them both. Though he would have liked to pleasure her until she came apart in his arms, he feared her poor head would suffer for the orgasm. Reluctantly, he moved his fingers to less volatile territory.

She smelled of exotic shower gel and honeysuckle shampoo. Unable to resist a taste, he caught one nipple between his teeth and tugged gently. Maria cried out, her face now flushed with wild color. "Alex, please," she begged, panting.

Temptation beckoned. The prospect of burying himself inside her and satisfying the craving that had built for weeks was almost irresistible. He could almost feel the warm clasp of her sex on his.

But when her fingers went to the buttons of his shirt, he stopped her, shuddering and dragging in great lungfuls of air as he struggled for control. "We can't. We can't. Not tonight."

Had she been a hundred percent, she would have done everything in her power to change his mind. He knew that. But she was weak and hurting, her energy at a low ebb.

Tears glistened on her eyelashes, making him feel like the world's biggest cad. "Go away," she cried.

That was one request he couldn't honor. He sat up, moving so that she rested her full length on her side with her head in his lap, her cheek on his thigh. Reaching for the remote, he backed to the opening scene and raised the volume. The film was a black-and-white classic.

He touched her forehead. "Rest, sweetheart. Please."

Though her eyes were open, he couldn't see her expression. For a little while, her body was tense, but gradually he felt her relax. When he thought she was half-asleep, he began to stroke her hair.

The experience changed him. He recognized the seismic shift and marveled at it. Work and pleasing his father had driven his life for so long he scarcely remembered any other way. But tonight…with Maria…he found himself yearning for something he couldn't even identify.

He had never considered himself a jealous man. The truth was, he had never cared enough before for such an emotion to be an issue.

Maria responded to him physically. There was no question of that. But she guarded her feelings and emotions. Did she want anything more from him than physical release?

The thing that bothered him the most was the notion that she might be eventually won over by the bad-boy prince, Gabriel. The other man was apparently irresistible to women. His exploits were the fodder of international gossip rags, even without a royal role.

Worse still was the inescapable truth that Gabriel liked and admired Maria, and vice versa. If such a relationship softened Gabriel to the notion of the Montoros reclaiming the monarchy, could Alex in all good conscience stand in the way? He had devoted weeks and months of his life and his career to affecting this change for the good of Alma.

If a match between Gabriel and Maria made the Montoros more receptive to the proposal, the smartest thing for Alex to do was step aside. But every cell in his body rejected the idea. He'd perfected the art of being a politician first and a man second. Now, integrity be damned, the idea was repugnant to him.

He was not here in Florida, however, to pursue his own agenda. He had been sent as deputy prime minister of commerce to solidify an ancient bond that would take Alma with confidence into the twenty-first century as a world player.

How could he betray the trust of his people for his own selfish ends?

At last, Maria's steady breathing told him she

was asleep. Her eyelashes, a shade darker than her hair, fanned out on her cheeks. He knew he probably should have made sure she iced her face, but in his urge to find intimacy with her, the thought had escaped him.

Now, he couldn't bear to wake her.

The medicine had done its work. When he eased out from under her and stood, she barely stirred. Unfortunately, her robe was still unbelted, her breasts bared to his hungry gaze.

Looking at her without her knowledge seemed wrong. Carefully, he tucked the garment around her and knotted the sash. Leaving her for a moment, he went into her bedroom and turned down the covers of her bed. He flipped on a small light in the bathroom and closed the door except for a narrow crack. She might awaken confused in the night.

When he returned to the living room, his heart contracted in his chest. She was smiling in her sleep. He would give a hell of a lot to know if he figured in that pleasant dream.

Gritting his teeth against the rush of need that assaulted him, he bent and lifted her carefully into his arms. Though her robe sheltered her now, he had a very good memory.

Maria was limp in his arms. He worried about that, but he had to trust that the doctor knew his business. Tucking her into bed, he adjusted the sheet and the light, summer-weight comforter. He doubted he would sleep much. Unappeased sexual arousal and a very real concern about Maria's injury guaranteed a wakeful night.

Pulling his phone from his pocket, he set the alarm. He would check on her every hour. She would never know, but it would give him peace of mind.

Maria stretched and winced as her head throbbed. Oh, Lordy. All of the events of yesterday came flooding back in living color...including the memory of Alex's big warm hands on her body.

She flushed from head to toe. And as she did, she grimaced when she realized she had no clue how she had made it from the sofa to the bed. Alex seemed to have a thing for carrying her, so that was a good guess.

Somehow, the thought of him looking after her

when she was asleep made her uneasy. Vulnerability was dangerous. She needed to be on her guard, because it would be a mistake to let Alex get too close until she knew what he had in mind.

A business-trip fling was one thing. His position was secure. She had the most to lose.

But what if he wanted more? Back in Alma life would revert to the status quo. Alex would continue to be wealthy and powerful and influential while Maria would go back to being the bastard daughter of a laundress.

That wasn't self-pity talking. It was simply the cold, hard truth.

When she climbed out of bed and stood upright, her head throbbed, but not too badly. The worst part was looking in the bathroom mirror. Holy cow. It was a good thing she had makeup with her. It was going to take a deft hand to ensure her face was presentable for a day with the Montoros.

A day with the Montoros. She chuckled out loud. That sounded like a television series. The trouble was, Maria didn't have the luxury of changing the channel. She had to dress and play her part. Even if today's agenda was ostensibly relaxation and recreation, she and Alex were still officially on the clock. Everything they said or did could have implications for the new regime. That responsibility was never far from her mind.

It took her a half hour to dress and cover up the worst of the bruising around her eye socket. By parting her hair differently and leaving one side loose to fall across her cheek, she managed to improve her appearance significantly.

The headache was bearable this morning, so she decided to skip the prescription stuff in favor of simple ibuprofen. Only then did she notice the small folded slip of paper on the bedside table.

Picking up the note with fingers that trembled, she opened it and studied the bold, masculine scrawl...

Gone up for breakfast at the main house. We all thought you needed to sleep more than eat. When you're hungry, the housekeeper has something fixed for you in the kitchen.
A

If she'd been expecting a tender missive, she was way off base. Not by any stretch of the imagination could the words be construed as personal.

And the "we all" was probably only Alex making his usual sweeping judgments, thinking he knew what was best.

Well, darn him, in this case he was right. It was almost ten-thirty and she was only now feeling halfway human and presentable. Given the late hour and the fact that lunch was not far off, she only nibbled at the beautifully prepared tray of food set out in the kitchen beneath a layer of thin linen napkins.

The kiwi and grapefruit and mangoes tempted her the most. And the pitcher of freshly squeezed juice. She did allow herself one of the small perfect cinnamon rolls, as well.

By the time she had eaten and brushed her teeth, there was still no sign of anyone coming to fetch her. Not willing to sit cooling her heels, she went outside and found that a golf cart sat waiting, key in the ignition. Mindful of Alex's alligator warnings, she eyed the open side of the low-slung vehicle with reservation.

But boredom and curiosity won out. She only took one wrong turn and recognized it immediately, so she was justifiably proud when she made it to the Montoro house without incident. The same dignified man from yesterday answered the door when she rang the bell.

Feeling unaccountably nervous, she followed him down the hall to the salon where she and Alex had met the family. Gabriel was the first to spot her hovering in the doorway. He jumped to his feet and met her halfway as she entered the room.

His hands on her shoulders, he cocked his head and studied her face, his own gaze anxious. "How do you feel, Maria?" Gently, he brushed aside a swath of hair to see the bruises she had tried so hard to disguise.

Even his gentle fingertip on her brow made her wince. "Much better," she said. "It's not so bad…honestly."

He kissed her on both cheeks in the European way and released her. "I believe you are a really bad liar."

Bella hovered, as well, surprising Maria with a quick hug. "I worried about you last night. I know the doctor said you didn't have a concussion, but they do make mistakes sometimes."

Being the center of attention was not a comfortable position, particularly with the entire Montoro clan in attendance. "I'm fine, really. But I appreciate your concern."

Rafael Montoro, the older, offered her a seat at his side. "We've been talking business. Alex wanted more information about our company's plans for expansion."

She glanced at Alex, perturbed to find his expression curiously blank. "I thought this was a social visit," she said, smiling.

Rafael nodded. "Bella just called us out on that very subject right before you arrived. I promised her no more boring talk today. I believe you young people are in for a treat. Gabriel has arranged for an airboat tour of the Everglades."

Maria clenched the arm of the love seat. "That's very kind, but I'm sure all of you have been there often. No need to play tourist for us."

Alex raised an eyebrow. He was standing near the window, one hand in his pocket. His posture was relaxed, but she knew him well enough to see the traces of tension in the way he held his mouth. "What Maria isn't saying," he drawled, "is that she is not fond of alligators."

Everyone looked at her, including Isabella. The older woman seemed taken aback. "It's entirely safe," she said in her quavering voice. "I used to love those trips when I was younger."

Even Rafe, Gabriel's brother, nodded. "It's a gorgeous day. You'll love it. I promise."

Juan Carlos chimed in. "Ordinarily, I'd be joining you, too, Miss Ferro. The trip will be delightful. Unfortunately, I have another commitment today. But you really have nothing to worry about."

Maria swallowed her misgivings, realizing she had no choice in the matter. "Sounds like fun."

Seven

Two hours later, after a sumptuous lunch of roasted pork and summer squash, Maria found herself with Bella in the backseat of a large, luxuriously outfitted van. Up front, Gabriel sat at the wheel with his brother in the passenger seat. Alex occupied the middle row, flanked by two large coolers filled with beverages and snacks.

Maria eyed the coolers with misgivings. Exactly how long *was* this trip? Eventually, they pulled into a nondescript gas station and met up with their guide, who then led them in his ancient pickup truck out to the docks where the boats were tethered.

On the upside, the airboats appeared to be modern and well maintained. The padded seats, three and three, were elevated to provide the best vantage point for viewing wildlife. But there was no railing of any kind.

Bella took her arm. "We'll give you the seat in the middle."

That was some small comfort. Maria had assumed Alex might want to sit beside her, but he joined Rafael in the other row. Leaving Gabriel to flank her opposite Bella.

When the guide handed out headphones to block the noise of the motor, Maria eyed her set askance, deciding that she'd rather be deaf than have that thing pressing on her injured head. Gabriel fished out a plastic-wrapped pair of earbuds from his pocket. "You may not need any of this. It's up to you. But I brought you these, just in case."

"That was sweet of you."

He shook his head ruefully. "Merely my guilty conscience at work."

As it turned out, the airboat was noisy, but not incredibly so. The pilot scudded rapidly through the waterways until they reached the Everglades proper. Now he slowed the pace, sliding over the surface of the water as they entered the grass-lands. Birds flew everywhere. One of the first varieties of wildlife they spotted in the water was not an alligator at all, but actually a banded snake that turned out to be very rare.

In the midst of the beauty and wonder of it all, Maria forgot to be afraid. Almost. The vegetation was lush and the heat oppressive. Before start-ing out, she had pulled her hair into a high pony-tail and donned a hat and dark sunglasses. Even so, the saunalike atmosphere was sweltering. Soon they were deep in a mangrove swamp. The creek they traversed narrowed in spots until there was barely room for the boat.

All the while she was conscious of Alex sitting behind her. What was he thinking? Maybe not about her at all. Perhaps last night meant noth-ing more to him than a bit of fooling around. The thought left a sick feeling in the pit of her stom-ach. And the taste of shame.

It was one thing to initiate something that might be serious, but another entirely to think that Alex saw her as an easy mark.

When Gabriel touched her arm, pointing out a bald eagle, she forced herself to ignore Alex completely. The Everglades were fascinating, 4,300 square miles, a river of grass…unlike anything she had ever seen.

Again, she asked herself why the Montoros would choose to go home to Alma. For the generation sitting in the boat today, Alma was no more home than it was to Maria. She had chosen to move there so she could keep her job when the Ramons relocated their oil business. But for Bella and Rafael and Gabriel, there was nothing but the history in dry books to tie them to the island nation. Who could expect them to tear up roots and make a new home four thousand miles away?

After they had been touring for an hour and a half, the captain steered the boat to a halt and tied it to an outcropping of bushes. Maria looked around with a frown. "Why are we stopping?"

Rafael spoke up. "We like to explore the island. You can get a feel for what it was like before humans came."

"Um, no thanks. I'll wait for you here."

The other four and the grizzled captain stared at her.

She shrugged. "I looked up fatal alligator attacks on humans on the internet yesterday afternoon. I'll be fine right here. I promise."

The captain chewed a toothpick in the side of his mouth. "Reckon you'll be safer on land. No gator's gonna go after six adults together. But one might take a notion to climb into an empty airboat."

Maria scrambled onto shore without another word, enduring the laughter that followed her. The men set up a folding table and some deck chairs. Their guide started opening the coolers and pulling out packets of boiled shrimp and French bread.

The meal had a surreal feel to it. Though Alex still avoided her, she found a quiet pleasure in the day. This trip to the States might be her last chance to travel for many years. Her position paid well as such jobs went, but if she planned to help her mother retire early, there would be little extra money, certainly not for worldwide jaunts.

The negatives facing her had piled up; the negotiations in particular were not going well. Alex was giving her the cold shoulder. She had a bruise the size of a small country around her eye, with a headache to match. But even so, she couldn't be sorry about today. The Montoros were fun and interesting people. She was seeing an ecosystem that was both fragile and starkly beautiful.

When the meal was finished, the Montoro siblings squabbled about how to pack up the leftovers. The guide headed back to the boat. For a moment, Maria and Alex were isolated in a bubble of silence a few yards away from the others. She summoned her courage and spoke her mind. "Are you angry with me, Alex?"

She saw a muscle in his throat work. "No. Of course not."

"You've barely looked at me all day. I can't help thinking the change in you is about last night."

Beneath his tan he was pale. He glanced around, perhaps hoping for rescue, but the Montoros were oblivious. "I don't know what you mean," he said.

Her temper flared. "Oh, please, Alex. Don't lie to me. Surely I deserve better than that."

He clenched his jaw, perspiration beading on his forehead from the thick, heavy air. "It isn't the time or place to talk about this."

"This what?" she asked, her gaze curious, though she knew exactly what he meant.

"We made a mistake," he said through clenched

teeth. His voice was low, barely audible. "We're here in Miami to do a job. We have to finish writing the proposal and we have to convince them to sign it. We don't have the luxury of…" He trailed off, but his meaning was clear.

"I see." Hurt made her breathless. Emotion stung the backs of her eyes, but she wouldn't cry. Her injury and her restless night had left her defenses at low ebb. "I won't mention it again. It was nothing anyway."

Alex watched her walk away from him and wanted to curse long and loud. The very thing he'd hoped to avoid had happened. He had hurt Maria, and all because he hadn't been able to resist touching her.

She joined the Montoro siblings, pitching in to clean up the last of the picnic debris. When Gabriel suggested a short walk, Maria nodded. That told Alex more than anything about the state of her mind. She would rather venture into a cypress swamp rife with alligators than remain in his presence one second longer.

He let them go, unable to stomach the sight of Maria's arm tucked in Gabriel's. As the foursome wandered off, Rafael and Bella joked about "*lions and tigers and bears, oh my.*" Gabriel merely kept Maria close to his side, promising to defend her to the death. His dramatic vow made Maria laugh. Alex kicked a root at the happy sound, his thoughts grim.

It was becoming clearer every day that Gabriel Montoro liked Maria. A lot. In a romantic way? Who knew...? But Alex needed to back off or risk damaging the relationships that were integral to the success of his mission for Alma.

As he sat on the airboat and listened to the old captain tell stories of the Florida that existed before Disney and the interstate highway system, only half of Alex's attention was engaged. He was debating his options. He could send Maria back to Alma on some pretext. That would put an end to his temptation, and she would also be out of Gabriel's reach.

But the idea lasted only a nanosecond. Maria was a gifted, hardworking member of the delegation, and she deserved this chance to shine. Alex had no right to kick her off the team; nor did he have the moral imperative to step in between her and Gabriel.

His conclusions were sound. But he didn't have to like them.

In another twenty minutes, the explorers returned to the boat, all in one piece as Gabriel pointed out, poking Maria in the ribs with a sly smile.

"No thanks to you," she said, settling into her original seat and sparing no glance for Alex.

The captain started up the boat, and the rest of the afternoon passed without incident. To Alex's critical eye, Maria seemed to flag by the end of the day, but he had abdicated any right to check on her well-being. When the Montoros dropped off Alex and Maria at the guesthouse, Maria disappeared into her bedroom without so much as a word.

Though they later rode in a golf cart together up to the main house, the journey was silent.

Dinner that night was both pleasant and awkward if such a thing was possible. Isabella was in attendance, her wheelchair pulled to the edge of the table at Rafael III's right hand. Her nephew encouraged her to tell stories of the old times, and the elderly woman did so with enthusiasm.

She'd had one of her rare good spells today.

Though her body trembled and her voice was weak, it was clear to everyone present that her spirit was unquenched. Isabella had been a very young child when the royal family was overthrown. In all likelihood, she didn't actually remember any of the details. But the tales of the traumatic events had been repeated often as she grew up, and to her, the end of the Montoro reign was still vivid.

Alex knew—as did her family, he supposed—that Isabella would not be happy until another Montoro ascended the throne that was rightfully theirs. She was in a fragile state. The span of her life was uncertain. What would happen if she died before a decision had been reached? Would the Montoro family choose to stay in Miami?

Alex had plenty of questions and not enough answers.

Gabriel asked Maria to stay for coffee after dinner adjourned. He glanced at Alex. "I'll bring her home before curfew, I promise."

Alex managed a smile, but his gut churned. Walking out of that house and leaving Maria with Gabriel was one of the hardest things he had ever had to do. The hollow feeling in his chest told him he was in deep trouble. He had been lying to himself about the intensity of his feelings for Maria.

With that knowledge came stinging regret. Had he crushed something new and beautiful beneath the heel of his duty and ambition?

He should have been proud of his dedication and resolve.

But it wasn't pride that kept him awake until three in the morning, when he heard the front door of the villa open and shut...

By Monday morning, Maria was able to conceal most of the vestiges of her contact with Gabriel's spiked volleyball. The swelling around her eye had gone down, and, with artful concealer, her appearance was close to normal.

She had never been more thankful for the presence of the lawyer, Jean Claude. Having a buffer meant that she and Alex were able to work side by side on the draft of the official proposition without acknowledging the events of the weekend. By noon, they were so deeply involved in the knotty questions of language and ceremony that personal situations were pushed aside.

The document was shaping up nicely. Alex and Maria were composing the actual words. Jean Claude was guiding them with the necessary legal language. The collaborative effort flowed well, though as Maria worked feverishly at her laptop, transcribing the conversations, she couldn't help but wonder if all of this would be in vain.

That night she ordered room service for dinner and fell into bed soon after, too tired from the intensity of the day's efforts to do more than dream of Alex. The same pattern repeated itself for the following three days. On Friday morning, the rough draft of the document was complete. Though satisfying, it was only the first step. It would have to be faxed to the prime minister back in Alma. In addition, the entire delegation was to meet the following week to pick it apart and look for weaknesses.

Unfortunately, Jean Claude received a phone call midday summoning him back to Alma for a family funeral. Harried and sad, he offered Alex a bulging folder. "You and Maria can handle editing and polishing over the weekend. Here are all my notes. I'll check in with you before Monday to see if you have any questions."

When he was gone, the silence in the room became oppressive. Maria swallowed hard. She and Alex had shared barely half a dozen personal words since the day of the airboat ride. She hated the rift between them. For years they had worked together in harmony.

Even when she was promoted to a new position and no longer reported directly to Alex, they still had frequent contact in the Department of Commerce. And of course, here in Miami, he *was* her boss. She had been thrilled to be picked for the delegation, especially knowing it would be a chance to work with Alex again.

Since coming to Miami, she'd seen him in a new light—in all honesty, as a potential lover. And it had seemed to her as if Alex was experiencing the same shift in dynamics. There was awareness between them. An unspoken bond that had bloomed out in the open in Miami's atmosphere of hedonism and fun.

Their first kiss had rocked her…had forced her to be honest with herself about the fact that her admiration for Alex had segued into something much deeper and more volatile. She wanted him.

When she was injured and he cared for her with such wildly intimate results, she'd been sure he was feeling the same desperate, crazy passion that she was. But almost in the next instant, he had shut her down. Which said that his emotions were unengaged.

He might have a physical response to her as a woman. But she needed and wanted far more. So much more.

"Shall we continue?" she asked. "With the editing, I mean."

His face was hard to read. "I think not. We've worked incredibly hard this week. Why don't we take the rest of the day for ourselves? Call a truce. Play tourist."

Her heart sank. He was offering an olive branch at the worst possible time. "That's very kind of you, Alex. And very tempting. But I'm meeting Bella and Gabriel and Rafe for an early dinner."

His dark eyes flashed fire for a brief second before his expression shuttered. "I see."

She shoved her hands through her hair. "No. I don't think you do. They're concerned about the future. And they know I'm not a native of Alma, so they think I can be objective."

"And can you?"

The derision in his voice hurt. "I've given a hundred percent to the work of the delegation. And I'll do everything in my power to convince them the monarchy is important for everyone."

"Anything else?"

The sarcasm was overt, but she was angry enough now not to be affected by his scorn. "If you must know, I'm trying to get closer to Gabriel."

"I'll bet you are."

"Oh, grow up," she said. "Somebody has to ferret out his bad-boy secrets, not to mention defusing anything that might embarrass the Montoros once they return to Alma."

"And that has to be you?"

"Do you have a better idea? He likes me. I think he trusts me. So I'm going to use that connection to do my job."

Alex's glare could have melted a Titanic-sized iceberg. He held up his hands, his cheekbones streaked with color. "Don't let me stand in your way, Ms. Ferro. Good luck."

Fury sent her across the room to go toe-to-toe with the irritating man. "I can't believe I ever thought you were a nice guy. You're overbearing, hostile, argumentative—"

He shut her up abruptly by the simple expedient of slamming his mouth down on hers. Neither suave nor sophisticated, the move reeked of desperation.

Shock held her immobile for two seconds before she put her hands on his shoulders in a token attempt to shove him away. "I won't let you kiss me," she muttered. But her arms curled around his neck and her lips parted to allow his tongue entrance.

She was so damned mad at him, but somehow all that feeling transmuted into hunger that consumed her from the inside out.

He wedged a leg between hers. "I don't know what to do about you, Maria. God help me, I don't."

With some last vestige of self-respect, she jerked out of his embrace. Her knees trembled, and she could barely breathe. But she wouldn't let him toy with her emotions. Not like this.

She wiped the back of her hand across her

mouth, trying to eradicate the taste of him. "You need to make up your mind, Alex," she whispered raggedly. "Either I'm a valued employee or a prospective lover or a gold digger looking to marry into the royal family. When you figure out the answer, be sure to let me know."

Walking toward the door, she stopped abruptly and gave him one last withering glance. "I'll see you here Monday morning at nine o'clock sharp. If you need any edits on the document over the weekend, email them to me. I think it would be better for everyone concerned if you and I stay away from each other."

Eight

By the time dinner rolled around Maria had run the gamut of emotions. She had burned with anger, cried with regret and at last found a certain measure of peace by reminding herself that she was only a small part of a much larger purpose. Her relationship with Alex, or lack thereof, was secondary to the job she had been engaged to do.

Alma, as a nation, faced a critical juncture. At such points in history, personal agendas often took a backseat to working for the greater good. This wasn't wartime, but in a sense, she and Alex were living in the midst of a volatile shift in national identity.

Reminding herself of what was at stake helped

put her own troubles in perspective. Broken hearts were a dime a dozen. She'd get over hers. Besides, it was probably only bruised. She'd had a crush. That was all…

Meeting Bella, Rafe and Gabriel in the hotel lobby was interesting to say the least. Paparazzi were not as ubiquitous in Miami as they were in some parts of the world. But the Montoros were both famous and flamboyant. The public enjoyed their antics…even more so now that gossip had begun to circulate about a possible tie to Alma.

Though Maria found it disconcerting when a camera flash went off in her face, the Montoro trio seemed to take it in stride. They had planned to walk the block and a half to their favorite seafood place. When it became clear to the guy carrying the camera that nothing too dramatic was afoot, he slunk away without further incident.

The restaurant overlooked the water and was crowded even at this early hour. Reservations required. When the Montoro party was granted a premium table near the window, Maria began to see that this branch of modern royalty was comfortable with the trappings of wealth and privilege. They might have to adapt to a new country and new titles, but theirs was no rags-to-riches story.

Over a meal that was exquisite in every way, her dinner companions grilled her about Alma and its current state.

She grimaced as she dabbed her lips with a linen napkin. "Where do I start? You'll be happy to know that the government has made technology a priority, both for education and in the private sector. Certain books and movies were banned under the old regime, but now information and entertainment flow freely."

Bella wanted to know about the palace. "Is it habitable?"

"Oh, yes. Tantaberra, and later his son and grandson, made themselves very comfortable over the years. Even during the revolt, little was damaged. Efforts are already underway to update the furnishings and to clean and remodel. I think you'll be pleasantly surprised when you see it."

Rafe frowned. "*If*, not when."

She felt her face heat. "Sorry. Didn't mean to get ahead of myself."

Gabriel appeared far more serious than she had seen him on other occasions. "Are the people really in favor of this move, or is it the brainchild of a favored few?"

"The press has done good job of advancing the idea. In a recent poll, seventy-two percent favored a return of the traditional monarchy."

Bella grimaced. "And what about the other twenty-eight percent?"

"Some of those are young people who are suspicious of anything that reeks of being told what to do and how to act. They want assurances of freedom and personal choice. Once they see that Alma functions well with the constitutional monarchy, I think the poll numbers will be even higher."

Rafe was still the quietest of the three. She couldn't quite tell if it was because of the situation or because his personality was more measured than his younger siblings. He lifted a shoulder, as if to say he was taking a fatalistic view. "In the end, what difference will it make if I say yes or say no?"

Maria started to respond with the official line but then pulled back and spoke from the heart. "I grew up in London. My mother and I had nothing. Every day was a struggle for her. But she adored the royal family. It was as if they represented something special about England that was a part of her, as well, though she was never likely to meet a royal or see one in person. I watched her swell with pride when good things happened to them and shake her head in grief when tragedies happened."

"Then why did you move away from England?" Gabriel asked.

"I had been working for Alex's family for several years when things changed in Alma and the Ramons decided to return to their homeland. My job paid well, far more than my mother was making. And in Alma I would have opportunities for advancement. So together, we made the decision to leave England. I can tell you, though, that she will be one to cheer the loudest if the Montoros return. She understands what the monarchy means to the common people."

The table fell silent. Maria hadn't spoken with the intent of making anyone feel sorry for her or her mother. But there could no longer be any doubt that the social chasm between the two Ferro women and the Montoros—or the Ramons, for that matter—was vast.

She couldn't decide if she had done more harm than good when her companions consumed their desserts in silence. Had she been too frank? Did they think she was too pushy? Should she have let more senior members of the team do the persuading?

At last, she pushed her plate aside, her lemon meringue pie only half-eaten. "One more thing, and then we can abandon this topic."

Gabriel shook his head. "Why stop now? You're on a roll."

"Very funny." She clasped her hands in her lap, feeling the damp palms that signaled her nervousness. More than anything, she wished Alex were here beside her. For more reasons than one. "Your family is very well-known in Florida, probably across the States, too. But the publicity storm that will be unleashed if you agree to reclaim your positions as royal family will be unprecedented. You think Prince William and Kate and baby George have been photographed continually? That will be nothing compared to your return."

Bella wrinkled her nose. "Surely you're exaggerating."

"I don't think so. We're talking about a throne that has been empty for seven decades. And a new king who is handsome and charismatic and single. Your whole family will be in the public eye."

Gabriel slumped back in his chair. "Oh, goody."

Rafe lapsed into silence. Bella excused herself to go to the ladies' room. Maria fixed Gabriel with a half-apologetic stare. "Part of my job is going to be media spin and public relations. Since you seem to carry the black sheep reputation, I have to ask…are there are any situations we will need to know about?"

His chuckle was dry. "To the best of my knowledge, I have no secret offspring hidden about the state. And no outstanding warrants. The worst of my sins are more gray than black. Wouldn't you agree, Rafe?"

His older brother grinned widely, for once looking almost carefree. "Far be it from me to weigh in on your confessional. But I promise, Maria, Gabriel won't embarrass us. He's too smooth and charming. If critics pop up, he'll simply woo them or schmooze them. They'll never know what hit them."

Rafe's assurances removed most of her concerns. Maybe Gabriel wasn't quite the loose cannon she had expected. Which was a good thing for everyone involved.

When Bella returned to the table, the group rose to leave. Bella and Rafael were headed out to a party. Gabriel offered to walk Maria back to her hotel. Along the way, she was startled when he opened up to her in a very serious voice. "I'm worried about my brother," he said, his voice flat. "I don't want him to give up his life."

"Has he said much to you?"

"Not really. But I found out today that he and my father have known about this monarchy thing for at least a couple of months."

"And you didn't?"

"No. Apparently the prime minister of Alma contacted our father and told him what was brewing…along with pointing out that Dad was not going to be king."

"That must have been an uncomfortable conversation."

"Indeed. Anyway, Rafael was sworn to secrecy until the delegation arrived. But it explains a lot."

"What do you mean?"

"Well, a few weeks ago, Rafe took off to Key West for an unexpected trip. I offered to go with him…we often fish and snorkel there together. But he told me no…that he needed some time alone to clear his head. At the moment, I had no idea what he was talking about."

"But now you do."

Gabriel paused in front of Maria's hotel. "Yes. Now I do."

She touched his arm. "You'll be a big help to him. Whichever way the decision goes. I can tell he thinks a lot of you."

"I appreciate the pep talk, Maria. It's no wonder Alex is madly in love with you."

"Excuse me?" She took a step backward in shock.

"Oh, come on. Surely you've noticed. Every time I get close to you, he practically bares his teeth at me."

Her head pounded and her chest tightened with anxiety. "You're mistaken. We're colleagues. That's all."

"Trust me on this one. I'm a guy. I know how guys think."

"He accused me of trying to cozy up to you so I could be a princess."

Gabriel laughed out loud. "And do you want to be a princess?"

"Not particularly," she said, truthful but wry.

He gave her an oddly sweet smile. "I think you and I will turn out to be good friends by the time this is all over. And I could use a friend right about now."

"You have a reputation for being a party lover. I find it hard to believe you don't have a confidante on every street corner."

"Plenty of women in my life. I'll admit to that. But they all want something. You're an open book, Maria. I like you a lot, even if we aren't romantically inclined."

"And Alex?"

He grimaced. "I don't have the same warm, fuzzy feelings about your boss. My family will tell you that I get a kick out of stirring up trouble. I could help you make him jealous."

"No, thank you." Imagining Alex's glacial expression if he thought Maria was encouraging Gabriel's interest made her cringe. "Besides,

I told him there was nothing between us but friendship."

"And did he believe you?"

"I don't know what he believes," she said, realizing that this was a highly inappropriate conversation to be having with a member of Alma's prospective royal family. "I should go now," she said quietly.

"I've embarrassed you. I'm sorry."

"No. I'm fine. But I shouldn't overstep my bounds. You and your family are very important to the future of Alma. I don't want you to think I take that lightly."

"No one thinks that, Maria. Believe it or not, none of us gives a damn about Alma's class hierarchy."

"You may not, but others do. I appreciate your taking the time tonight to let me talk to you. Please reiterate my thanks to your brother and sister."

"So formal. So serious."

She knew he was teasing her, but she was suddenly desperate to regain some sense of formality between them…as if Alex could see the fact that she and Gabriel were comfortable with each other. "Good night, Gabriel," she said.

He watched her walk up the steps. "It will all work out, Maria. Things always do."

"I hope you're right."

Alex paced the confines of his hotel room, feeling the walls close in around him. It had been eight hours, give or take, since he last saw Maria. If she had her way, the two of them wouldn't meet again until Monday morning when they were surrounded by the Alma delegation.

He had handled things with her poorly from the beginning...probably, because for once in his life, he didn't have a clear idea of how to proceed. Not in regard to the proposal and the Montoros. That path was well defined. It was his personal life that seemed out of control. Hell, up until the past few weeks, he hadn't even allowed himself to imagine a personal life that included any woman on a permanent basis.

But with Maria at his side and under his nose day in and day out, it was becoming increasingly difficult to convince himself that he was a patriot first and a man second.

He glanced at his watch. It was late, but not too late. He wasn't going to be able to sleep unless he saw her. That in itself was disturbing. They had known each other for a long time now. Had worked together in a number of settings. When had things started to change? When had he begun to notice the way her smile hit him in the gut? Or been stricken with the need to touch her? To make her laugh?

Grabbing up his key and his phone, he strode across the room. But when he jerked open the door in preparation for leaving, Maria stood in the hallway, her hand raised to knock.

Her arm dropped, and her eyes widened. "Alex."

He pulled up short, his adrenaline-fueled momentum stymied by the fact that she had come to him. "Maria."

To an outsider, the tableau would have seemed comical. Maria recovered first, already backing away. "You were going out," she said. "I can talk to you later."

He grabbed her arm and dragged her inside, closing the door firmly. "No. We'll talk now."

"But—"

He put a hand over her mouth. "I was coming to find you," he said gruffly.

Maria freed herself from his loose hold and moved to stand beside the window. "If you're going to yell at me again, I'd just as soon pass."

He shook his head. "I didn't yell."

"What would you call it?"

"Mutual aggravation?"

That coaxed a smile from her. "Fair enough."

"Why did you come to find me?" he asked.

"I wanted to let you know how the dinner went."

His chest tightened with disappointment. So much for the personal agenda. "Okay. Let's hear it."

"May I have a seat?"

"Of course."

They moved to the nearby grouping of sofas and chairs. The room was extremely large. Though Alex hadn't asked for it, he presumed that his position as head of the delegation had warranted the generous quarters.

Maria was dressed casually in a soft multi-colored skirt that touched her knees and a thin, sleeveless top of ivory silk. The barely there sandals she wore showcased pink toenails.

Although she sat on the love seat, he was too antsy to join her at the moment. He ran a hand through his hair. "So tell me. How did it go?"

She shrugged, her expression pensive. "It's hard to say. They asked a million questions. Good questions. Rafe, as always, was reserved."

"Do they seem at all receptive to the proposal?"

"They're guarding their options. We have to remember that they haven't even seen a copy of it yet."

"True. If the rough draft gets an okay next week, the plan was to go ahead and let the Montoros take a look."

"Does that mean they get a chance to approve or disapprove?"

"I don't think the delegation will like that idea. Unless we have a solid commitment first."

"In other words, two stubborn entities in a standoff."

"No one wants to lose face or operate from a position of weakness."

"I think the key to winning them over is going to be the personal touch. If they trust you and the delegation, they're going to be much more likely to agree to our proposal."

"Well, they trust *you*. That's a start."

She crossed her arms and thrust out her chin. "There you go again. Flinging insults."

He held out his hands. "I certainly did not. It was a compliment."

Her expression was skeptical. "Didn't sound like one."

Judging himself sufficiently in control of his emotions to get closer, he sat down beside her and touched her arm. "I'm glad they feel comfortable talking to you. Really I am. You're an incredible asset to the team."

She stared at him, vulnerability in the depths of her gaze. At times he forgot about her humble beginnings and that her maturity belied her years. "I'm serious," he said softly. "I admire you, Maria. You're smart and quick-thinking and you have a better grasp of human emotions than I do. Thank you for meeting with Rafe and Bella and Gabriel tonight."

"You're welcome," she said, her words barely audible.

She no longer met his gaze, so he had to lift

her chin with his finger. "I don't like it when we fight," he muttered.

Maria didn't reply, but her hand came up to cover his. He thought she meant to push him away, but instead, she twined her fingers with his. "I don't like it, either."

Ten seconds passed. Or maybe a hundred. Awareness quivered in the air. He could hear the thump of his own heartbeat in his ears. Maria's cheeks flushed, her eyes starry with something he dared not put a name to. Later, he couldn't remember which of them moved first.

Their lips met softly…tentatively. He slid a hand beneath her hair to cup the back of her neck. The top of her spine was fragile, the curve of her nape feminine. "I want you," he said. He had an advanced degree in diplomacy and a reputation as a persuasive leader. But in that moment he felt as awkward as a high school kid on his first date.

Maria leaned into him, her posture both eager and trusting. He should try to be worthy of that trust, but if such a thing meant sending her away, then he was doomed.

She put a hand against his cheek, stroking the stubble that appeared if he didn't shave twice a day. Her gaze clashed with his, her eyes deep enough to drown in. "I want you, too, Alex. But without regrets. If this time in Miami is all we have, let it be enough."

Nine

The wording made him frown. What she was offering would be the perfect scenario for most men. A temporary liaison. No strings attached. Yet, oddly, her plea unsettled him.

Because he didn't want to answer, he let his actions tell her what he couldn't yet say. The silk shell she wore came off easily over her head. He caught a ragged breath at the sight of her breasts barely covered in smooth, ivory satin. When he tossed the top aside, he realized that his hands were shaking.

Maria had gone still, her wary gaze alert, like a doe in the forest scenting danger. But she didn't stop him when he drew her to her feet. "I need you naked," he groaned, unzipping her skirt and drawing it down and off. Her French-cut undies matched the bra. Plain...unadorned...but sexy as hell. "Ah, Maria."

She hadn't said a word since he began unwrapping the most wonderful present he'd ever been offered. Was it shyness that kept her silent?

"I don't know what you're thinking," he muttered. The bra fell away. He steadied her as she stepped out of the sandals. Tracing the elastic band of her only remaining item of clothing, he sighed. "Please say something."

Her smile was tremulous. "I haven't done this very often."

"I don't need an accounting." In fact, he'd rather not know. The thought of his Maria with other men made him a little crazy.

"That's not what I mean." She started in on his shirt buttons. "I want to please you. But my experience is—"

He put a hand over her mouth for the second time that night. "Your experience is irrelevant. That's what it is...irrelevant. Neither of us has ever been here before. Everything we say and do in this room is brand-new." He tucked her hair aside and kissed the soft skin beneath her ear. "Brand-new, Maria."

It took a great deal of fortitude to allow her to unclothe him. But she was so sweetly intent on her task he clenched his fists at his hips and let her take the lead. When her fingers touched his belt buckle, he inhaled sharply, the sound a quick hiss of startled shock.

Since when had a woman ever been able to arouse him with such innocent motions? Stretched on a rack of unfilled desire, he braced himself as she slid his shirt from his shoulders and then tugged his trousers to his knees. When she paused, he kicked off his socks and shoes and pants in one ungainly dance.

His navy boxers did little to hide how much he wanted her.

And still his would-be lover was mute. "I think we could adjourn to the bed," he said, smiling with a grimace that was supposed to be reassuring.

Maria nodded, allowing him to take her hand and draw her toward the king-size mattress that could sleep half a dozen men. The coverlet was navy damask, the contrasting pillows and trim taupe. Against the heavy, ornate fabric, Maria's skin would glow.

At the last instant, he picked her up in his arms and used one hand to fling back the covers. Maria looked up at him, her eyelashes at half-mast, her throat and chest flushed with color. "I'm on the pill," she said.

All members of the delegation had undergone fairly stringent physicals before leaving for the States. Though he had condoms with him, he found himself fiercely glad that they would be unnecessary.

"Are you sure?" he asked hoarsely. "I don't want you to think I'm coercing you."

For the first time since she entered his suite, her face lightened, and she laughed out loud. "I'm pretty sure you're not. It's a little insulting that I had to work so hard to get your attention."

He deposited her on the soft sheets and followed her down. "Are you kidding? I noticed you the first day you came to work for our company in London. But you were way too young and I was way too busy."

"And later?" Her arms remained at her sides, as if she were afraid to move.

He traced a fingertip from the center of her forehead, down her nose, between her breasts, all the way to her navel, where he stopped to let both of them catch their breath. "In Alma I watched you bloom from a pretty young girl to a mature, fascinating woman. But we were both consumed with the work at hand—steering Alma's fate."

"Did you have this in mind when you suggested me to be on the delegation?"

Her quiet question caught him off guard. He was the one to flush this time. Had he envisioned this moment? Really? It troubled him that he couldn't give her an unequivocal answer.

She stroked his collarbone with both hands, moving down his chest as he leaned over her on one elbow. "It doesn't matter," she said. "Because even if you didn't, I did. I've had the worst crush on you. Then somehow, when we got to Florida, everything got worse."

"Worse? Or better?" He lightly rubbed her nipples one after the other, breathing harder when she arched off the bed and called his name.

This time…this precious first time. He knew he wanted it to be special for her, but lust rode him like a wild animal, consuming everything in its path. Honor…tenderness…gentle care.

Maria trembled against him, as nervous as a wide-eyed cat. "Relax," he muttered. "I won't do anything you don't like." But when he buried his face between her thighs and feasted on the taste of her, nothing short of cataclysm could have made him stop before he pushed her off the edge of a choked climax.

"More," he groaned. "We'll do more later. But I can't wait."

He felt the last flutters of her climax against his shaft as he pushed his way inside her. The tight fit…the heat…all of it overwhelmed him. Because in the midst of intense physical euphoria he felt something else. A notion that terrified him and made him weak.

He might be in love with her.

Maria still reeled in the aftermath of what had been an unprecedented orgasm. She'd been sure such things were the stuff of movies and books. Who could believe that the earth actually rocked on its axis when the right man staked a claim?

Alex filled her completely, in a way she barely

understood. He was a man with all the usual equipment, but even in her limited experience, she recognized that this was something far beyond a casual hookup. Maybe not for him, but certainly for her.

And because she had courted this moment, watched for it, waited for it to happen, she would be the one with the most to lose. Alex Ramon was not available for everlasting love. He was smart and wonderful and passionate, but he was not hers.

That dreadful reality refused to take root in light of the fact that he was thrusting inside her wildly, rolling to his back and encouraging her own acrobatics. "Take what you want, Maria. Take it all."

His breathless grin encompassed a masculine satisfaction that should have made her want to smack him for his impudence...if she hadn't been trembling on the brink of yet another exquisite climax. "Who's taking whom?" she asked primly, stingingly aware that he felt larger and more determined from this angle.

"Doesn't matter." He groaned when she dared to reach behind and touch the base of his erection.

Where his fingers gripped her buttocks, she would likely have bruises tomorrow. She looked down at him, seeing the power in his broad shoulders, the pleasing symmetry of his pectoral muscles, the sleek delineation of his rib cage.

"You are a beautiful man," she breathed, squeezing inwardly as he dragged her down onto his hard flesh again and again. "I never knew what you were hiding beneath all those hand-tailored suits."

His head pressed into the pillow as he gasped. "Well, we're even then, because I may never let you get dressed again."

With one last twist of his hips, he took them both into the deep end. As the wave crashed over her, violent and deeply satisfying, she slumped onto his chest and counted the beats of his heart.

Alex couldn't feel his legs. Paralysis was, as a rule, a frightening state. But at this particular juncture in his life, he couldn't bring himself to care.

Maria slept like the dead, her limp body draped over him as the softest, sweetest of blankets. Her hair was in his mouth and his nose, and one of her knees threatened his male anatomy. But all he could do was smile and thank his guardian angel for arranging this tryst.

Did angels even know about sex? Well, of course they did, because it was pretty clear that he'd just caught a glimpse of heaven.

His feelings were all over the map. Since he was not a man to even recognize the fact that he *had* emotions, the sharp shift in outlook was both alarming and bemusing.

Maria. It was all about Maria. Offstage, problems loitered, ready to shatter his giddy, post-coital bliss. But he refused to countenance them. One night. One mad, insanely wonderful night. That's all he wanted, all he asked for. When the sun rose, he would pick up the reins of civic obligation once again.

But tonight was his. His and Maria's.

He woke her with a kiss. A kiss that started with a quick nibble on a tender earlobe and ended up with her stretched out on her back, his teeth raking the spot where neck and shoulder met.

"What are you doing?" she mumbled, refusing to open her eyes.

"If you have to ask, I must be doing it wrong."

"Alexxx…" Two syllables stretched to the breaking point.

Her shoulder was particularly sexy. How had he never noticed that? "You're sweet and soft and I want you more now than I did a half hour ago."

"Is that even possible?"

He choked out a laugh, trying to decide what he should taste next. "Look at me and tell me you feel it, too."

Long lashes tipped in gold lifted. Her irises were more blue than green right now. Her pupils were dilated. She was sated and drowsy and completely irresistible.

When she licked her lips, he could swear it was unconscious…that she had no clue what that little movement did to him.

"I should go to my room, Alex."

He frowned. "Why?"

"We have to be circumspect. You're a very important man. Gossip could be detrimental to your career."

"Screw my career." How could she even think like that? They were naked and wrapped in each other's arms. It pissed him off that she had the presence of mind to be concerned about propriety.

She feathered the fingers of both hands through his hair, sending a shiver down his spine. "Be sensible, Alex. Please."

"I'm *always* sensible," he said through clenched teeth. "I'm sick of being sensible. As far as I'm concerned, you're not leaving this room until Monday morning."

"What about the editing and revising?"

Bless her wonderful, conscientious, puritanical heart. She was trying to save him from himself. "We both have laptops. No one expects to hear from us tomorrow or Sunday. It's the perfect scenario. I'll make love to you until neither of us can breathe, then we'll order room service, work on the document a bit and go back to bed."

"You're serious…" Her gaze searched his face, looking for God knows what.

Even he could see that his behavior was an anomaly. His father would be horrified. But his father was far, far away, and Alex was in the midst of a sexual awakening of unprecedented proportions.

What if sex with Maria was more than scratching an itch? What if this was what he'd been missing his entire adult life?

She exhaled, perhaps signaling capitulation. "I'd still have to go to my room and get a few things. What if someone sees me?"

"We're on the same floor. Opposite halls, granted...but it will be a quick trip. Quit worrying."

At long last she nodded slightly. "Okay."

When she climbed out of bed and began to search for her clothes, he was stricken with the notion that she might not return. He took her chin in his hand and stared into her eyes. "You won't change your mind?"

He'd meant the words to sound like a command, but they came out closer to a plea than he would have liked.

Both of them were naked. Upright. He could lift her and take her again right now. The image made him breathless.

"I'll come back," she said.

As a bit of insurance, he confiscated her bra and undies and stuffed them in a dresser drawer. "I want you to think of me when you're walking half-naked down the hall."

"I can't do that," she said, her expression aghast. "What if someone sees?"

"I suppose you'd better hurry."

* * *

Maria scuttled down the carpeted hallway, her arms wrapped around her waist. The building was air-conditioned to arctic levels, and she knew her bare breasts were noticeable beneath her thin top. The knowledge made her face hot, but not as much as reliving what had just transpired in Alex's suite.

If she had not promised to return, there was a good chance she would have avoided him until Monday. Could he read her that well?

Once safely inside her own room, she rested her back against the door, breathing rapidly. She was not the kind of woman who had affairs right under the noses of people who knew her…who expected her to be hardworking and ethical and dedicated to Alma's cause.

Were all those expectations in her head? Maybe people were just people…fallible, unable to predict, good and bad.

Wanting Alex as a lover didn't negate her contributions to the work of the delegation. As a group, the delegation had been sent to Miami with express instructions to take the weekends off. Healthy, productive humans knew how to relax. So why was Maria freaked out about the notion of being spontaneous and irresponsible with Alex Ramon?

Avoiding her own question, she found a straw tote that looked more like a purse than a suitcase and began stuffing it with essentials: toiletries, clean undies, her billfold, a comfy pair of yoga pants and a loose cotton top. The paperback novel she was in the midst of.

On second thought, she took the book out of the bag. Chances were, Alex didn't plan to give her much opportunity for reading.

When she had rounded up everything she thought she might need for the weekend, she stared at the perfectly made bed. *Damn.* She wasn't cut out for a life of deception and hanky-panky. Placing the tote beside the door, she set to work making the room look lived-in.

She tossed the covers until the bed was a tumbled mess. Then she went into the bathroom, dampened a towel and washcloth and crumpled them on the floor. Finally, she opened a packet of soap and wet it before placing it in the shower.

Feeling more than a little ridiculous, she examined her quarters with an eagle eye. The delegation was well-known already, at least within the hotel. Service workers noticed all sorts of intimate details. Maria wanted to make it perfectly clear to anyone who might be paying attention that she had definitely slept in her own room, tonight...*not* in room 1724.

Grimacing at the realization that she would likely have to repeat this same charade tomorrow afternoon, she shook her head at her own foolishness and decided she had kept Alex waiting long enough.

Opening the door to the hallway a crack, she gazed left and right. No one in sight. Though she managed to hold up her head and walk with confidence down the corridor, around the atrium and back to the far wing, her heart was beating so rapidly she felt dizzy.

When she knocked on Alex's door, and he opened it immediately, she practically fell into his arms. "No one saw me," she whispered.

Alex was dressed again...in the same clothes he had worn earlier, minus the shoes and socks. His bare feet were long and sexy.

He took her shoulders in his hands, looking at her with alarm. "You're shaking, Maria."

"Adrenaline," she said on a sigh, thrusting her bag into his arms and dropping into an armchair. "I think I need a drink."

He poured her a glass of white wine and crouched at her side, his warm, dark eyes dancing with amusement. "If I had known it was such a big deal, I would have gone to your room myself."

She raised an eyebrow. "And let you riffle through my unmentionables? I don't think so. We don't know each other that well."

He stroked a finger down her arm, making her shiver. "I've seen you naked," he said solemnly. "I think I'm allowed to touch your underwear."

"It's a slippery slope. First it's the underwear and next thing you know you'll be asking me to spend the night."

His chiseled, masculine lips quirked. "I think I already did."

She stared at him moodily. They were so close at this angle all she had to do was lean forward three or four inches and she could touch her mouth to his. "Do you really think we can concentrate on work in between…um…you know?"

His breath was warm on her cheek. "I have no

idea. But I'm willing to find out. Besides, we're supposed to be taking the weekend off."

"Doesn't matter. You and I both know that we have to make sure the proposal is ready for the briefing."

"We'll get it done, I promise. I work best under pressure."

"And what if we can't stop having sex? What if we ravage each other 24/7 until we barely know if it's day or night?"

Ten

Alex's erection had abated during Maria's absence. But if she planned to say things like that to him, how was he supposed to keep his head? His imagination exhibited a sudden astounding propensity for cinematic sexual fantasy. Clearing his throat, he rose to his feet and put some distance between them. "I suppose that's a risk we'll have to take."

The chair was oversize. Maria had curled her legs beneath her and huddled into the depths of the cushions until it seemed as if she were trying to become invisible.

Small, perfect white teeth mauled her bottom lip. "You're not taking me seriously."

His hoarse chuckle was strained. "I've never been *more* serious. But I'd feel a whole lot better if you weren't regarding spending two days and nights with me as the equivalent of going in for a root canal. Sex is fun, Maria."

"Not with you."

She'd spoken rapidly and with conviction. Without the hint of a smile on her face. "I'm almost afraid to ask you to elaborate," he muttered, telling himself grown men didn't get their feelings hurt.

Maria's hands gripped the arms of the chair, her knuckles white. "It wasn't fun earlier. Earth-shattering, maybe. Mind-blowing. Unequivocally wonderful. But not *fun*. That's a word for carnival rides and animated movies and walking barefoot in the rain."

Her earnest speech might have been good for his ego if she didn't seemed so distressed.

He scooped her out of the chair and sat back down with her in his lap. "You're overthinking this, Maria." He nuzzled her ear. "Maybe we didn't start with fun. I'll give you that one. But we'll get there. Eventually. Good sex, I think, hits all the positive adjectives eventually."

She sighed, resting her cheek against his heart. "Have you had *bad* sex?"

"Enough to know the difference." He stroked her hair. "Trust me, sweetheart. Trust *us*."

"You make it sound so easy."

"And you're making it far too complicated. We're here in this room. A man and a woman. Attracted to each other. Unattached. With time on our hands. What makes you think something bad is going to happen?"

"Superstition?"

He laughed ruefully. It was hard to argue the point that the old ways in Alma were laden with superstition. Legends. Folk tales. Fables delineating the fates of those who tempted the gods. Alma's was a culture steeped in centuries of oral tradition.

"You're a thoroughly modern woman. We're here representing the best and brightest of a country eager to make its mark on a new millennium. Relax. There's nothing to worry about."

"I think it's all those years of my mother warning me that misbehavior on my part would have drastic consequences. It was a very effective deterrent."

"I'll protect you if the sky starts to fall."

"Not funny."

He tickled her rib. "A little bit funny. Admit it."

Her body relaxed in his embrace. They had broken some awkward barrier and made it safely through to the other side.

She put her hand on his thigh. "Did you mention room service?"

Alex watched Maria eat a strawberry and was forced to lean forward to lick juice from the slope of her breast. "I'll order more of those," he promised.

They were both naked. It was three in the morning, and they had chosen to shore up their energy with a snack of fresh fruit and champagne.

Maria's hair tumbled around her shoulders. Dark smudges beneath her eyes attested to the fact that so far he hadn't managed to let her sleep for more than thirty minutes at a stretch.

How could he? When she nestled close to him, her bottom cradled against his groin, he wanted her again and again.

More juice dribbled onto her cleavage. "You're doing that on purpose," he accused.

She eyed him innocently, her lips closing on a bite of red berry. "Are you complaining?"

"Hell, no." This time when he licked her velvety soft skin, he shuddered. "We need to sleep." His hands were at her hips, tugging her down onto the mattress. He had no intention at all of closing his eyes.

"We can sleep when we're dead," she said, the words slurred with exhaustion. She was so beautiful in her sensual abandon that it hurt to look at her.

Those six words were all the invitation he needed. He eased her onto her side facing away from him. Lifting her leg over his thigh, he entered her from behind, joining their bodies with an ease that made his head swim. This was so perfect…so right.

Maria's head rested on her arm.

"Are you asleep?" he asked, smiling though she couldn't see him.

"Just catnapping. Keep up the good work."

"I never knew you were such a smart-ass," he teased. He withdrew and thrust firmly, burying himself all the way to the hilt and making each of them gasp in unison.

"I've been on my best behavior at work."

"Will you be insulted if I say I like this version of you even more?"

He curled an arm around her hip and reached for the spot that controlled her pleasure. Toying gently with the small nub, he slowed his penetration to enjoy her restless arousal.

"Not insulted," she moaned. "Don't stop."

He felt his climax bearing down on him and willed it back. "What will you do for me if I let you come?" he asked, the words ragged.

"Anything, everything. Damn you, Alex. Please..."

She tried to twist in his embrace so she could face him, but he held her firmly. Already he felt small contractions in her sex that told him she was close, so close. "I like it when you beg." He bit the back of her neck. "Will you let me kiss you in public?"

He didn't even know where the question came from...hadn't realized he was about to ask it.

Maria stiffened, the small shake of her head unmistakable. "Not that. Nothing out in the open. I'm offering you this room, this weekend, these two nights. Anything and everything. No holds barred."

Though her words promised a sexual carte blanche, he was pissed at her refusal to have a real relationship with him in the light of day. Really pissed...but not enough to let her go. "Fine." He forced the word past clenched teeth. "But I'll make you pay for that."

He couldn't wait any longer. Cursing softly, he released the tight control he'd maintained and plunged wildly, taking her again and again with a force and fury that rocked the bed and sent them both into a fiery crash with orgasmic pleasure so intense they collapsed instantly into a deep, sated sleep.

Maria awoke completely disoriented. For a split second she thought she was in her small apartment in Alma. Then gradually, everything came back to her, including the fact that a large, naked man held her tightly with both arms locked around her even as he slept.

For a moment, she remained still, struggling to assimilate everything that had happened. Fragments of memories...pieces of the night before, sent hot color to her face and made her wonder how much was dream and how much reality.

But when Alex murmured in his sleep, his face buried in her hair, she couldn't pretend any longer. She and Alex had made love...repeatedly. And the experience had changed her forever. She had given him a part of her soul and it wasn't something she could or would take back.

Panic rose in her chest. She had done the one thing she knew was dangerous. She had let Alex get too close. It wasn't just the sex, though that was bad enough. But even worse, she had let down her guard with him...let him see who she really was.

Whatever professional distance had existed between them had been obliterated in one unprecedented night. Alex clearly wasn't alarmed by that. He seemed to have some notion that it was no big deal.

But Maria knew the truth. Soon they would return to Alma, and there it would be impossible to continue whatever this was between them. Alma was struggling to assimilate the fast-moving future with their traditional past, but it was a struggle that would take more than a week or a month or even a year. In the meantime, the old lines of class and social standing would remain mostly intact.

Not only was Maria not a native of Alma, she was a woman with no past. No father, no relatives, no lineage. Only a hardworking mother who had done her best to keep food on the table.

Oh, what the hell. Just because heartbreak lurked around the corner, it didn't negate the benefits of a weekend in bed with the man she lo—

She pulled herself up short. *Love* was an inappropriate word in this context. She wasn't in love with Alex. In lust maybe. But who could blame her? He was smart and sexy, and underneath that oh-so-serious exterior, he was an animal.

Even so, one of them had to show some sense. Carefully, over the space of at least a minute and a half, she stealthily eased out of his embrace and off the bed. Poor man never even moved. He had expended an impressive amount of energy in the past twelve hours.

Maria's insides clenched in helpless longing as she remembered the crazed fervor of his love-making. He'd been like a man possessed, as if trying to make up for lost time. Or maybe, deep down, he knew as she did that their time together was limited.

In the bathroom with the door closed, she showered, dried her hair and secured it at the back of her neck. The comfy clothes she'd grabbed while in her room last night would be perfect for an informal workday.

She'd expected to find Alex awake by the time she finished. Opening the door to the bedroom stealthily, she saw that he still slept. Only now, he was facedown on his stomach. His broad, muscular shoulders and smoothly tanned back narrowed to a taut waist and buttocks that were… well…it was a good thing the sheet hadn't slid any lower.

She jumped when low, amused words startled her. "Are you going to stand there staring or are you going to come back to bed?" He reared up on one elbow and turned to look at her. His voice sounded as if he had swallowed sand.

"It's nine o'clock. We need to order breakfast and get to work on the proposal."

He sat up and scrubbed his hands through his hair, yawning. "Are you always so perky at this hour?"

"If you're trying to make me mad, it won't work. Tell me what you want to eat and I'll have it waiting when you get out of the shower."

When he swung his legs over the side of the bed, she held up a hand. "Wrap the sheet around you, for heaven's sake."

He stretched, the muscles in his broad chest doing some kind of mesmerizing flex and ripple. "Are we shy this morning?"

"Not at all," she said primly. "But we don't need to get sidetracked. There's work to do."

He stood up, sans sheet, and crossed the room in three long strides. Putting a finger beneath her chin, he tilted her face up to his, searching her eyes. "You okay, sweet thing? We got a little crazy last night."

She couldn't do a thing about her blush, aggravating as it was. "I'm fine. Better than fine. But seriously, Alex. It's late. One of us has to remember why we're here."

He kissed her long and slow, telling her in no uncertain terms what he thought of her work ethic. Her arms went around his neck and clung. Every inch of his big, honed body pressed against hers, stealing the oxygen from her lungs.

When he finally released her, she had to grab hold of him for a few seconds until her world settled back on its axis. "Stop that," she whispered, going up on tiptoe to kiss him again.

His low, triumphant laugh was masculine arrogance personified, but she couldn't fault his confidence since she was clearly besotted. Did anyone even use that word anymore? If not, they should. It was a perfect description of her current state. Intoxicated. Infatuated. As if all her good sense had flown out the window, and she didn't even care.

But she could pretend. Releasing him reluctantly, she took a deep breath. "More kissing later. Go, Alex. Now."

He bowed, managing despite his nudity to look perfectly relaxed. "Far be it from me to argue with a lady."

When he disappeared into the bathroom, she exhaled, not realizing she had been holding her breath. Dealing with Alex in his current mood was like trying to tame a big, determined tiger.

While he was gone, she escaped to the living room. After a moment's consideration, she moved the vase of fresh flowers from the cherry writing desk. Opening the drapes that framed a stunning view of the Atlantic, she dragged the ornate table in front of the window. Next, she located both laptops, plugged them in behind the new workspace, booted her computer and opened up the rough draft of the Alma proposal to the Montoros.

Once that was done, she called in two orders of scrambled eggs, bacon and black coffee. Room service at this hotel was extremely efficient. She didn't want the food to get cold.

She would have liked to sit down and start working to show Alex that she was taking their new relationship in stride, but it was impossible. She paced the room. Today was a watershed moment for her and Alex. She recognized the importance of what would happen in the next few hours. So she felt a certain amount of pressure to guard her emotions.

Alex was a guy. He was going to have one thing on his mind. Despite his position as deputy prime minister of commerce, he would be able to compartmentalize. Sex wouldn't interfere with his position or his responsibilities.

But for Maria, life wasn't so clear-cut and simple. Could she have an intimate physical relationship with him and still be able to carry on with business as usual when they were with other members of the delegation?

She was so deep in thought that she never heard his footsteps on the plush carpet. When his hand landed on her shoulder, she spun around. "You scared me," she said, not quite able to meet his gaze.

"Who were you expecting, Maria?"

A knock at the door saved her from answering. "I'm going in the bedroom," she whispered. "I don't want anyone to know I'm here."

Alex shook his head with a wry smile but let her go.

When he gave her the all clear, she returned to a beautifully laid out breakfast. Linen napkins, real silver utensils, crystal stemware and delicate china. "That smells wonderful," she said as her stomach growled audibly.

He held out her chair, leaning down to kiss her cheek. "Looks pretty damn good, too."

Fortunately for her peace of mind, Alex was content to eat in silence. They were both starving. He caught her eye at one point and grinned,

as if to say he knew exactly what she was thinking. She hid behind a cup of hot tea and wondered
how long it would be before they ended up back
in bed. *Bad Maria*, her conscience chastised.

But apparently, she had convinced Alex of her
dedication to the project at hand. Once they were
done with their meal, he carried his coffee to
the desk where she had placed two chairs side
by side.

"How do you think we should approach this?"
he asked, waking his own laptop and clicking
on a file.

His matter-of-fact attitude took her aback.
She'd been prepared to convince him, to deflect
amorous advances. Was he genuinely so cavalier
about working with her?

When he burst out laughing, she stiffened.
"What's so funny?" she demanded, finishing her
tea and standing up. She couldn't quite make her
feet move in his direction.

"You," he said, his smile gentle. "You told me
we had to be all business this morning. But when
I took you at your word, you were disappointed."

"No, I wasn't," she said. The rebuttal wasn't
convincing, even to her.

"Well, I am," he said firmly. "We're going to get this done as quickly as possible so I can get you back in bed."

Her spirits lightened. "You must think me awfully naive, Alex. I'm not accustomed to combining business with pleasure. This is new territory to me."

He frowned, leaning a hip against the desk. "What do you think it is to me? I don't make a habit of sleeping with coworkers. In fact, you're the first."

"Why me?"

"I could ask you the same thing," he said, watching her with a hooded gaze. "If you want explanations, I'm fresh out."

"So where and how do we go from here?"

"Does everything in life have to be explained? Let's file this thing between us under the same category as raindrops trapped in cobwebs or the color of the sky at dawn."

Her eyes widened. "Why, Alex, I never knew you were a poet."

His expression was impassive, not a trace of humor in sight. "There's a lot you don't know about me, Maria. So how about giving both of us a chance to learn something and possibly to be surprised?"

There was an odd tone in his voice, some tiny indication that he was not as certain as she thought he was about what had happened between them last night.

It was then she realized she wasn't being fair. Either she was in this, or she wasn't.

It took courage, but she walked to where he stood and slid her arms around his waist. "I've been second-guessing myself, Alex. But that's over. I'm content to take things one day at a time. I can't guarantee I'll be able to work with you and not want to jump your bones, but I'll try."

He hugged her so tightly she thought her ribs would crack. "God, Maria." He pulled back and rubbed his thumb over her cheekbone. "I thought I might have scared you off."

Eleven

"I don't scare that easily, Mr. Ramon."

"Thank God." Her cheeky grin was adorable. Alex felt as if he had dodged a bullet. There had been women in his life who had walked away. At least one or two. But none whose defection had given him heartburn.

This morning when he woke up alone, his heart had gone cold until he heard faint sounds from the bathroom. In those moments when he thought she had fled to her room, he'd felt a little sick. Not for anything in the world would he have her feel uneasy about what had happened between them. He decided then and there that if she wasn't a hundred percent on board with this new slant to their relationship, he wasn't going to chase after her. Not because of any pride on his part, but because Maria was too nice a woman to have to fend off unwanted advances from a coworker.

He wrapped a hand in her silky hair, wishing he could take her hard and fast, but they had reached a tentative accord. Maybe he should show some restraint. "I suppose we need to work," he said, finding little enthusiasm for the prospect.

"Definitely," she said. "And if we get a lot done, we might have time for some recreation later."

Alex replayed that promise repeatedly over the next three hours. It wasn't easy to stay focused, but he tried. Fortunately, once they delved into the draft of the proposal, he was able to keep his attention mostly on the words they were shaping rather than the scent of Maria's hair.

It touched him that she was so sweetly intent on their task. Though not a native of Alma, she took her responsibilities very seriously. The powers that be had been right to include her in the delegation.

The opening language of the proposal was flowery and formal, based mostly on historic documents. From there, Alex and Maria struggled with the order of points relating to the royal family's return. Should the legalities of power and function be first, or was it more politically correct to mention the palace and what was left of the Montoro fortune from before Tantaberra's regime?

At least they had Jean Claude's extensive notes when it came to lawyer-speak. Neither Alex nor Maria was trained in such areas. But they were both good editors, Alex catching the occasional typo and Maria smoothing out style and syntax.

At one in the afternoon, he called a halt. Standing behind her chair, he put his hand on her shoulders. "My eyes are crossing. We've done enough for now. I need food, woman."

"But we only have—"

He put his hand over her mouth. "It's for your own good, Miss Ferro. I'm seeing symptoms of workaholic-itis. It's a terrible disease and one that has to be nipped in the bud."

She stood up and stretched. "You're so full of it. But yeah…I guess we should stop. What do you want for lunch?"

He took her hand and reeled her in, tucking her

against his chest and resting his forehead against hers. "You," he muttered. "Only you."

They eventually got around to ordering pizza. Alex threw on some pants to answer the door and tip the delivery guy, but undressed again quickly so he could eat naked in bed with Maria.

"This is really a smart idea," she said, rescuing a blob of tomato sauce from her bare arm. "I don't have to worry about spilling anything on my clothes."

Alex nodded solemnly. "All part of my plan to keep you here indefinitely as my sexual plaything."

"Plaything?"

"What?" he asked. "You don't like the word?"

She pursed her lips, curling her tongue to rescue a string of cheese. "I was thinking more along the lines of erotic goddess."

He reclined on both elbows, suddenly uninterested in pizza. "I stand corrected," he said huskily.

Maria dabbed her lips with a napkin and frowned at him. "Stop that."

"Stop what?"

"Undressing me with your eyes."

"Um…I'm pretty sure that's not a fair rap. You're buck naked, my sweet. Or hadn't you noticed?"

She crossed her arms over her chest. "A gentleman wouldn't say things like that."

He grabbed her ankle and pulled, laughing when she pretended to struggle. "Then I guess I'm no gentleman."

Maria felt as if another woman had possessed her body. A female who was sexy and fun and carefree. Maybe she was channeling a 1940s film star. Glamorous. Mysterious. Living on the edge.

Alex's head rested on her bare belly, his hair tickling her leg. She stroked the outside of his ear. "You amaze me," she whispered. Her back rested against the headboard. As she cast her gaze over the bed, the view almost made her laugh. All the covers were on the floor. She and Alex lay sprawled on top of the fitted sheet.

She might have been cold if the man's body hadn't radiated heat like a furnace.

He yawned. "Amaze you how?"

"The whole Clark Kent/Superman thing. I've

worked *for* you and *with* you for years and only this weekend have I discovered all your super-powers."

"Maybe not all," he said, his smug, masculine grin rekindling a slow burn in her secret feminine places. "I just might have a few more surprises up my sleeve."

"Bragging isn't attractive, Alex." She squeezed his bicep. "And I might point out that you don't have any sleeves."

He pretended to frown as his hand roved her bare thigh, sending gooseflesh all over her body. "Details, woman. Details. You need to look at the big picture."

She brushed his erection with a fingertip. "Oh, I'm looking," she said.

When he laughed, she felt a jolt of pure happiness. Alone in this room, he had shown her a glimpse of the kind of relationship she had always wanted. But the Alex with her now didn't often come out to play.

He was dedicated to his country and to his responsibilities and to his role as deputy prime minister of commerce. The livelihoods of common people rested in his hands. He wielded tremendous talent and carried a tremendous load.

Alex sat up and hooked a hand behind her neck to kiss her. "Pepperoni," he muttered. "My favorite."

Suddenly, she was painfully aware of the ticking of the clock…of the invisible hourglass whose sand was draining away at an alarming pace. "Make love to me, Alex. I need you."

Neither of them noticed or cared when the pizza box fell to the floor. Alex's warm hands on her body caressed and petted and stroked and generally drove her insane. He liked to torment them both, to reduce each of them to desperation before finally moving over and into her with a slow, firm thrust that forged a connection she'd never known or understood.

Her body seemed already to recognize his…

The weight of him pinned her down. Her fingers clenched on his back, searching for purchase in the gathering storm. With her legs wrapped around his waist, she canted her hips, trying to force him deeper.

Alex gasped, his skin damp, his gaze unfocused. "I can't get enough. It's never enough…"

She knew what he meant. In the breathless moments after climax, she was as eager for him as she had been before he first touched her. Clinging to him as if he might be wrenched from her arms, she relished his hard frame, his hair-roughened arms, his male scent.

Everything about him was so different from her body. She was tall and strong, but in his embrace she felt the sweet vulnerability of a woman whose man wants her beyond all reason.

When they both crested at almost the same moment, a rush of moisture in her eyes caught her by surprise. There was nothing to cry about... nothing at all. She would carry the memories of this weekend with her for the rest of her life.

They dozed again for maybe an hour and then rose to finish their work on the draft. Finally, when they were both satisfied, Alex emailed the document to Jean Claude for his perusal. If everything passed muster, Alex and Maria would meet with the delegation on Monday morning to go over the proposal step by step.

After that, it would be up to the Montoros...

Alex stretched, his face shadowed by a day's growth of beard. "How about a walk on the beach? As much as I love hiding out in this room with you, I could use some fresh air."

"Definitely." They both slipped on the clothes they had worn Friday evening. Spending a naked weekend had definite pluses…less laundry to worry about.

She lobbied for leaving the room separately, but Alex put his foot down. "You're being silly. I'll check the hall if it will make you feel better, but we're not going to skulk around like we're doing something wrong."

Nevertheless, Maria was relieved when they took the back staircase and made it outside un-observed. They traversed the path to the sand in single file. When they reached the beach, Alex took her hand.

Her fingers linked with his as they meandered down toward the firmer sand revealed by low tide. They were not the only night owls out and about, but there was plenty of privacy for a pleas-ant stroll.

The moon hung low on the horizon, casting a silvery path across the sea. Maria wanted to capture the moment somehow. A photograph wouldn't do it justice. And she was no good as an artist. The fragrance of night-blooming jasmine scented the air. She would have to rely on imagination and sensory recall to hold on to this memory.

Alex adjusted his stride to hers, keeping the pace relaxed.

She felt her muscles relax, her misgivings washing away in the waves that curled onto the shore. "Have you ever wanted to buy a boat and sail toward the unknown?" she asked, not pausing to consider whether he would think her question a bit odd.

"Every boy dreams of that, I think…at least the ones who have seen the ocean. What did you want to be when you were a kid?"

"Oh, that's easy…a Disney princess."

"Which one?"

"Ariel and Snow White were my favorites, but the hair color was all wrong. My mother bought me a very beautiful Cinderella doll the Christmas I was six years old, and after that, Cinderella was the one I wanted. I carried her everywhere and decided I could be just like her when I grew up. Little girls' dreams are silly, I guess."

"No sillier than boys who want to be soldiers and firemen and police officers."

"But those are attainable goals. A girl can't actually grow up to be a princess. Unless, of course, you're Kate Middleton or someone like that."

Alex told himself not to read too much into her innocent confession. There were a million little girls around the world who wore princess outfits for Halloween costumes and considered sparkly tiaras a vital accessory. It didn't mean a thing.

Still, the evening lost some of its bloom.

They walked for half an hour and then retraced their steps. Afterward, Alex hailed a cab out at the street, despite Maria's insistence that they were far too messy to go anywhere.

But when she saw the all-night diner, her protests died. They binged on chicken-fried steak and homemade mashed potatoes. Alex tried to coax her into apple pie, but she shook her head.

"I'm stuffed," she said. "But you go for it."

When the dessert arrived, Alex forked up a generous bite and held it out to her. "At least taste it."

Staring at him with a small smile that made his

skin tighten on the back of his neck, she leaned forward and opened her mouth, allowing him to feed her the rich mix of fruit and spices and crumbly crust.

After she swallowed, a look of bliss crossed her face. "Oh, my gosh. That's amazing."

"More?" Her sensual enjoyment made him shift restlessly in his seat. He did a quick calculation of how long it would take to get back to the hotel.

Maria leaned away and shook her hand. "I can't. We've eaten like kings since we've been in Miami. I don't want to go home with an extra five pounds."

He finished the pie rapidly and lifted a hand for the check. Outside, he pushed her against the side of the building and kissed her wildly, his breathing ragged. "You're perfect the way you are," he muttered. "And I want you…now."

Fortunately, good sense prevailed and he managed to make it back to his suite before getting Maria naked. Little bits of sand showered down onto the carpet. "We should take a shower," she said. "So we won't get sand in the bed."

Nodding jerkily, unable to speak, he dragged her toward the bathroom, aware all the while that

Maria was laughing at him. He undressed her in record time and adjusted the water temperature before ripping off all his clothes. Even now, he could see that she was a little shy.

"Look at me, Maria." He took her hand and pulled her beneath the spray. The water darkened her hair immediately and dripped from the tips of her breasts. It was always a toss-up as to whether her eyes were going to be more green than blue. In the tiled shower stall with cavorting dolphins and wave motifs, her irises gleamed pale emerald.

She cast her gaze downward. "I'm looking, Alex. Believe me, I am."

When she wrapped one hand around his aching shaft, his head dropped back against the wall of the shower. *Holy hell.* Her fingers explored him above and below, making sweat break out on his forehead. His knees quivered embarrassingly. "Enough," he croaked.

When she tried to soap him up, he had to intervene. A man could only stand so much torture. "You first." Gliding his hands over slick female flesh made him shake again. He took care of his own ablutions and then hustled them both out of the shower, handing Maria a big fluffy towel.

Perhaps she'd been expecting him to suggest shower sex standing up, but he wanted her to be comfortable with him. Baby steps. Build her trust and her comfort level. Sooner or later she would feel at home in his arms and in his bed. He was counting on it.

By the time they dried off, he had convinced himself not to pounce on her. While he and Maria had walked the beach earlier, housekeeping had been in to service the room. The bed looked inviting, the covers pristine.

Maria, with the towel wrapped sarong-style around her torso, cocked her head. "Almost seems a shame to mess it up."

"What did you have in mind?" he asked, his hands fisting at his sides.

She pointed. At the foot of the bed stood a narrow cushioned bench. Instantly, he saw the possibilities. "I like the way you think." He dragged it away from the footboard and tested the springiness of the navy padding with two fingers. "Bottom or top?" he asked with a straight face.

Maria turned cherry red from the edge of the towel to her hairline. "I'll leave that up to you."

It was so much fun to tease her. She did her best to be nonchalant about what they were doing, but that shy reserve was never far below the surface. He ditched his towel and stretched out on his back, his feet on the floor. The height was perfect. His arousal was out in the open, his shaft full and heavy as it bobbed against his abdomen.

He held out a hand. "Come and get me," he said.

She kept a death grip on the towel, though she did walk a few steps in his direction. Her attention focused on his eager sex, but her expression was hard to read.

"I may have been too hasty. I like having covers to hide beneath."

"You're exquisite," he answered, dead serious. "It would be a crime to cover that gorgeous body. Drop the towel, sweetheart."

For a moment he thought she was going to refuse. But gradually, she unclenched her fingers and lifted her arms until the large, damp rectangle fell to her feet.

Alex sucked in a sharp breath, feeling the last bit of blood in his head rush south. "I'm cold. Come warm me up."

At last, a small smile. "You're never cold. And besides, I'm not exactly sure how to go about this."

"I'll help. It's like riding a bike. You never really forget."

"You're a riot," she said, biting her lip.

In the end, she started at his knees, straddling him with ladylike grace and *walking* up his body until his erection and her soft, damp sex were aligned. He grabbed her hips. "See…that wasn't so difficult."

Leaning forward, she put her hands on his shoulders and lowered herself onto him. They both made a noise halfway between a curse and a sigh. Her silky wet hair fell around them. He was conditioned by now to the smell of her shampoo. It made him want to gobble her up.

He didn't move for a few moments, giving her a chance to adjust to this new position. "You okay?" he asked. Her silence always bothered him. He never knew what she was thinking.

Maria did a little bump and grind with her hips that made him catch his breath. "I don't know," she muttered. "You tell me."

Twelve

Maria had taken a gymnastics class in college to satisfy a PE requirement. Nothing she learned during that semester prepared her for this current experience. Technically, she was in the dominant position. But in reality, Alex called the shots.

She had no objection to that at all. For one thing, she didn't have the sexual confidence yet to orchestrate their coupling. And for another, he was so damned good at sex. Feeling like a rank novice, she squeezed her inner muscles. When he gasped, she smiled.

"I like having you at my mercy," she said, her words little more than a whisper. She kissed him teasingly, nipping his bottom lip with her teeth. His response was to thrust upward…hard.

His hands tangled in her hair, anchoring her head so he could drag her mouth to his and hold her captive. In between kisses, his ragged, breathless praise seduced her. "You wanted to be an erotic goddess, right?"

She barely had the oxygen to answer. "Not really. That was just me being silly."

"Too bad," he groaned. "'Cause you're already there. Sit up," he said urgently.

When she did as he asked, the feel of him inside her was indescribable. Now she could see his face. His cheekbones were ruddy with color, his thick, inky-black hair mussed. He stared at her in return, capturing her attention with nothing more than the hungry look in his eyes.

"Lean back," he demanded. "Put your hands behind you on my thighs."

She obeyed, feeling intensely vulnerable and wildly excited at the same time. He cupped her breasts in his hands, teasing her nipples with his thumbs until the pink rosebuds puckered tightly.

Unable to bear the intense tableau, she closed her eyes.

"Look at me, Maria." The note of authority brooked no opposition. "Do you like what I'm doing to you?"

She tried to swallow. But her throat was dry. "Yes."

He plucked at her sensitive flesh, sending dual arrows of fire arcing to the spot where their bodies were joined. "Alex…" Her sharp cry echoed in the silent room.

His laugh encompassed masculine triumph and sexual intent. "Don't close your eyes. Keep watching."

He found her pleasure center and stroked the tiny bud carefully. When she jerked away instinctively his hands clamped on her hips. "Ride me, Maria. Make me come. I dare you."

The game was on, but she was so lost to reason she barely had the presence of mind to understand what he was saying. Bracing her feet, she pushed off from the floor, and came down hard. Her climax hit with the force of a tidal wave, tumbling her in a maelstrom of confusion and sharp physical pleasure.

Alex went wild beneath her, ramming into her

repeatedly, then shouting as he exploded inside her, filling her with his release.

She slumped on top of him, her heart beating loudly in her ears. Beneath her cheek, his chest was damp and *his* heart sounded as if it might leap out of his body.

"Are you good at *everything*?" she muttered, still half dazed.

Long seconds passed when she wondered if he was going to answer. Finally, he stroked her back, his words gruff. "It's you, Maria. You inspire me."

Afterward, she was never sure how long they lay there recovering. But her butt was chilled and her legs ached by the time Alex finally stirred. "Sleep," he said groggily. "We have to sleep."

They stumbled into the bathroom for a quick, strictly platonic shower. Then, with a nod to brushing teeth and a halfhearted attempt by the both of them to tame her hair, they finally gave up and went to bed. The sheets were cool and crisp and heavenly soft.

Alex wrapped an arm around her and tucked her against his side. She thought he was already asleep, so it startled her when he whispered something in her hair.

"I want to keep seeing you when we go home," he said.

She froze, resenting him for introducing conflict in the midst of their wonderful aftermath. "You'll see me every day," she said. "We work in the same office."

"That's not what I mean and you know it."

"Don't ruin what we have," she pleaded. "We can talk about it later."

Alex felt the rejection and marveled that something could be so painful. Was this all a game to Maria? Was he entertaining her while she waited for her chance with Gabriel? Had the little girl who wanted to grow up to be a Disney princess suddenly realized she had a shot at the real thing?

He didn't want to believe it. But he had no idea what it meant to come from nothing, to struggle financially, to feel the constant ache of uncertainty in every aspect of life. How could he fault her for seeking out financial security and a fairy-tale ending?

Or maybe it was Gabriel. Maybe Gabriel was

pursuing her so convincingly that she had to consider what it might mean to be a princess in real life. Alex had money to burn, but he was never going to be a prince. And because of the delicate state of the negotiations, he couldn't stand in the way if Gabriel wanted Maria.

She seemed naive sexually, as if there had been no more than one or two men before him. He didn't think she could fake the satisfaction he had given her. But why else would she hold him off if it weren't for the fact that she had plans to continue a relationship with Gabriel Montoro?

Unless, of course, she was worried about what might happen when she and Alex returned to Alma. Back home, their relationship had been circumspect and businesslike. Maybe Maria didn't want to juggle the inevitable gossip that would ensue if they returned to Alma as an official couple. He could appreciate her reservations even if he thought they were unfounded.

Despite his unsettled thoughts, exhaustion claimed him at last. But his dreams were fractured and troubled and kept him on the run all night.

* * *

Maria was sleeping like the dead when Alex's cell phone woke them at seven the next morning. He rolled over and groaned, picking it up to look at the number. Clearing his throat, he punched the button. "Ramon here…" He listened intently. "Yes, of course. Thanks for calling."

Maria sat up, clutching the top sheet to her breasts. She raked her hair from her forehead. "Who was it?"

He rotated his head as if trying to shake off the remnants of too little sleep and too many bad dreams. "It was Rafael Montoro—father, not son. Isabella Salazar has been admitted to the hospital. He wanted me to know, because it may affect our plans to formally offer the proposal to the family this week."

She touched his arm. "Oh, Alex. I'm so sorry."

He avoided her attempt to comfort him and climbed out of bed. "I think I should go to the hospital. As a show of support."

"I'll go with you." Her gaze searched his face.

"Suit yourself," he said. His tone was curt.

The laughing, playful, sexy lover of last night had disappeared. Was it because he was stressed about this turn of events? Or had she angered him by refusing to talk about their relationship beyond this room?

She didn't have the nerve to join him in the bathroom. So she gathered her things and waited until he was finished to take her turn. "I'll be very quick," she said.

He nodded without looking at her. "I'll wait."

As she quickly ran through her morning routine, she wondered if she had hurt his pride. It was too soon for his heart to be involved. But perhaps he was offended that she hadn't jumped at his offer to continue their sexual adventures, even back in Alma.

She would have liked to return to her own room for fresh clothing, but she was pretty sure Alex wouldn't linger. Not in the mood he was in. So she put on the same skirt and sleeveless silk top and examined it in the mirror. Not too bad.

Alex had used the time she was in the bathroom to order toast and coffee and request a car. They ate in fifteen minutes and headed downstairs to the lobby. Although she tried twice to engage him in conversation, Alex was stone-faced.

The hospital in Coral Gables was brand-new

and extremely high-tech from top to bottom.
Isabella's condition required intensive care, so
the family was gathered in the adjacent waiting room. While Rafael III conversed with Alex,
Maria sat with Isabella's grandson and the nieces
and nephews.

Juan Carlos was the one Maria knew the least.
His face was pale, his posture tense. "I'm sorry
about your grandmother," she said.

The young man inclined his head. "Thank you,
Ms. Ferro."

His manner was formal but polite. Suddenly,
his facade cracked as he glared at Rafe. "It's your
fault, damn it. She's upset because you won't live
up to your responsibilities."

Gabriel bristled. "It's not our country, and it's
not Rafe's burden to bear. Back off."

Bella, with a worried look at the stricken Rafe,
stepped in to make peace. "We're all upset. Snip-
ing at each other doesn't make it better." She sat
down beside Rafe and leaned her head on his
shoulder. "Isabella is old and sick and frail. We've
all known this day would come."

Rafe jumped to his feet, his eyes stormy with

something that looked a lot like fear. "She's not dead yet. And Juan Carlos is right. I was dragging my feet about this decision. I should have said yes or no and ended this."

Gabriel cursed, a vicious nasty word that encompassed the whole of the Gordian knot that bound them all together. "I need some air," he said.

Maria sensed he was close to the breaking point. He was either going to punch out his cousin or start tearing up the hospital brick by brick. Part of her job was to maintain control of the situation. The last thing they needed at this point was a media circus.

"Mind a little company?" she asked. She wasn't intentionally trying to make Alex jealous by slipping away with Gabriel. She was simply doing what needed to be done. But despite the purity of her motives, Alex shot her a narrow glance that telegraphed his disapproval.

Gabriel shrugged. "Not at all."

Bella gave her a grateful smile. "I'll text you if there's a change."

Outside, in the hospital courtyard, Maria sat on a concrete bench while Gabriel paced. The air was thick and humid, but it was still early enough that the temperature was bearable.

She searched her social repertoire for the right words to defuse his tension but came up with nothing. So she sat in silence. Finally, after fifteen or twenty minutes, he plopped down beside her. "It's a hell of a situation."

"I know. I'm sorry."

Gabriel leaned forward, his head in his hands. "If it were anyone else, I'd say my aunt was faking to manipulate my brother. But she's one of the most honorable women I've ever met."

"And passionate about her homeland."

"Yeah."

"The delegation is set to do a final read through of the official proposal tomorrow. After that, they'll want to meet with your family, or at least Rafe."

"Poor bastard."

"I'm guessing from what he said just now that he hasn't made up his mind?"

Gabriel shook his head. "Damned if I know. Rafe can mimic the Sphinx when he wants to… but this situation with Isabella makes things harder for him."

"Unless he had already decided to accept."

"I wish I had your positive attitude."

The irony was almost amusing. She didn't feel positive about anything at the moment.

"We probably should go back inside," she said. The sharp edge of Gabriel's anger had been dulled by acceptance and grief. Grief for both his aunt and his brother.

Maria stood up. Gabriel followed suit, shoving his hands in his pockets. "I don't suppose you'd help me run away to Tahiti in a sailboat and tell everyone I'm never coming back?"

She chuckled, liking him more and more each time they met. "You'd regret it if I said yes. Besides, the women of Miami would never forgive me for allowing South Beach's most eligible bachelor to disappear."

"Rafe's the one who's going to be a king. Doesn't that put him at the top of the eligible list?"

"Good point."

They were playing a silly game, trying to take their minds off the very serious events at stake. But nothing could disguise the truth.

She sighed. "You may not be the king," she

said, "but you know you can't run away, sailboat or no sailboat. Your family depends on you. Now more than ever. Bella is awfully young. Juan Carlos doesn't have a dog in this fight. And Rafe... well, he's under so much pressure. You can be the glue, Gabriel. They need you desperately, no matter what happens with Isabella."

He cocked his head. "You really care, don't you? About a group of strangers?"

"I've been studying dossiers on each one of you for months. I felt like I knew you before I arrived. But dry facts can only tell so much. Now that I've become acquainted with all of the Montoros, I can see the big picture. And I understand why you're important to Alma." She paused. "To be honest, I think Alma will be important to all of you, as well. But that's something you have to decide on your own."

He hugged her briefly. She felt a faint tremor in his body. There was nothing the least bit amorous about their quick embrace. Gabriel was simply a man at the end of his rope trying to hang on.

When he released her, his expression was sheepish. "You won't tell anyone I freaked out, will you?"

"Of course not. I think you're entitled."

He nodded once, his chin outthrust. "Enough of this. You're right. Let's go back in and see where things are."

Alex saw them move, so he stepped quickly around the corner of the building, unwilling to be discovered. The tableau he witnessed had filled his throat with bile. Despite the fact that Maria had spent the better part of the weekend in Alex's bed, there was no denying the truth. She and Gabriel were in the midst of something.

Body language didn't lie. They were comfortable with each other. Intimate. A connection like that could only happen when two people were very close.

Alex had known Maria for years and yet had never ended up in her bed until now. Gabriel had known her for a couple of weeks, and already the two of them were confidants. Maybe they hadn't had sex yet. Alex didn't honestly think Maria would sleep with two men in the same interval.

But she was not a hundred percent sure about her feelings for Alex. She was worried about how their relationship would play out back in Alma.

In some ways, Gabriel must have seemed to her like the easier choice. Or maybe Gabriel represented a walk on the wild side without consequences that would follow her home.

Alex felt the sting of betrayal even as he recognized his response as irrational. He and Maria had made no pledges. They were not exclusive. She had every right, moral or otherwise, to develop a relationship with Gabriel Montoro.

Alex scraped his hands across his face and reminded himself that this changed nothing. Isabella was still desperately ill. The proposal still had to pass muster with the delegation...then the Montoros. And Alex was still the orchestrator of everything.

Bleakly, he stared at a brilliant hibiscus that bloomed riotously in the Florida sun. He'd made a misstep. A bad one. But the situation could be rectified. It *would* be rectified. For a brief moment, he had broken his own personal code. He'd forgotten his responsibilities. He'd let personal desires outweigh the import of his position as head of the delegation.

But it wouldn't happen again.

He braced himself to return to the ICU waiting

room, barely able to tolerate the idea of Maria and Gabriel being chummy. But when he walked in, Gabriel and both Rafes were deep in conversation on one side of the room. Juan Carlos had apparently gone downstairs for something to eat. Bella and Maria had their heads together, their expressions grave.

Alex took a chair that wasn't close to anybody and pulled out his phone to check messages. He managed to concentrate for five minutes before stealing a glance at Maria. She was wearing the same skirt and top she'd had on when she came to his room. The same ones from their beach walk.

But all he could see was her naked body stretched out beneath his…her beautiful eyes laughing up at him.

When a nurse entered the waiting area, the anxiety level in the room went up half a dozen degrees. The woman spoke quietly to Rafael III. Then the head of the Montoro family looked at Maria and crooked a finger.

Maria stood, a puzzled expression on her face. "What's wrong?"

Rafael had aged a decade during this crisis,

his face gray with fatigue and worry. "My aunt would like to speak with you."

"I don't understand. Why me?"

"I don't know. But she's in a fragile state, and if she wants to talk to you, you will go to her."

The firm tone brooked no opposition.

Maria's panicked expression was genuine. "I'd like someone to go with me."

"I'll go," Alex said.

Maria's look of relief should have been gratifying, but he could scarcely bear to walk by her side.

The room was only steps away. The nurse halted them before going in. "She's somewhat agitated. But she said it was important."

Alex and Maria nodded.

When they opened the door, Alex lowered his voice and whispered in Maria's ear. "I'll be here with you, but I'll stay out of her line of sight. I don't want to upset her if she wants to be alone with you."

Maria's lips trembled. "This makes no sense."

He touched her elbow. "Just go."

Maria approached the bed slowly. "Mrs. Salazar. I'm here. It's Maria."

The old woman was too weak to lift her head, but she smiled. "Thank you for coming, my dear."

"Is there something I can do for you?"

Isabella's skin was sallow and her eyes were sunken. But her smile was a semblance of its original beauty. "I need you to tell me the truth. Is my great-nephew going to accept the crown?"

Maria shot Alex a glance, and he saw her swallow. "Well, ma'am, I believe he's still thinking about it."

"You had dinner with the children. All of them except Juan Carlos. Is that correct?"

"Yes."

Alex wanted to smile at the thought of the Montoros being referred to as children, but he listened to hear what Isabella would say next.

The matriarch was physically weak, but her formidable spirit survived intact. "Why are they so reluctant to accept their birthright?"

Maria bit her lip, her hand reaching out to clasp one of Isabella's. "You should know that they love you very much. And they respect your opinions and wishes. But what you're asking them to do is huge. They were born in this country. They're citizens of the United States. They have business interests and friends and a whole life here."

"That's why I wanted to talk to you," she said with the faintest of twinkles in her eyes. "I knew you wouldn't sugarcoat the truth."

"I'm not saying they won't decide to reclaim the monarchy. I honestly don't know. But for this whole situation to work…both personally and politically, it's my belief that Rafael will have to embrace the throne wholeheartedly or not at all."

The room fell silent. Alex frowned, wishing Maria had been more conciliatory with a patient at death's door.

Isabella squeezed Maria's hand. "I understand what you're telling me. I let my enthusiasm run amok, I think."

"Your feelings are understandable. You were born in Alma. You actually lived there. And your life was torn apart and rebuilt. Everyone values your experience. If it's any consolation, all of them are taking this very, very seriously. The decision may or may not fall the way you're hoping, but I can promise you this…Rafe will do the right thing. He's decent and thoughtful and well aware of the choice being offered."

"But the right thing may not be the throne." Isabella's lips twisted in a wry half smile.

"No, ma'am."

Alex stared at the monitors, waiting for them to go berserk as the elderly woman's blood pressure shot up or down or she flatlined. Maria had just crushed Isabella's dreams.

But the miraculous happened. Nothing changed. At least, not for the worse. Isabella reached out with a trembling hand and found the button that operated the hydraulics of the bed. Adjusting the mattress until she was partially sitting up, she lifted Maria's hand, kissed it and released her.

"You may go now. Please ask all of my family to come in and see me."

In the hall, Maria slumped against the wall, her face pale. She stared at Alex. "Don't make me do that again."

"No one forced you to go in there."

"It's not like I had a choice, and you know it."

He followed her around the corner and found the Montoros waiting anxiously. Maria grimaced. "She wants to see all of you."

When the room emptied, only Alex and Maria remained. He stared at the floor, his hands in his pockets. After a moment's reflection, he retrieved his room key and handed it to her. "Why don't you go on back? I can deal with things here."

"You're angry."

He shrugged. "Not angry. Maybe a little surprised. I saw you with Gabriel in the garden, Maria. And I understand why you hesitated when I mentioned continuing our fling."

She winced at the last word, her eyes wide with distress. "I swear to you, Alex, there's nothing going on between Gabriel and me."

"It's possible you honestly believe that. But I saw the way you two acted with each other, the body language. My personal feelings don't enter into this. If Gabriel has feelings for you, then I, as the head of the delegation, owe it to my country to step out of the way."

Color flushed her cheeks. "So now you're pimping me out for national security? That's insulting and horrible."

"Don't overreact. We can both be mature about this. You and I had a fun weekend. But we're in the midst of a crisis. It's very clear to me that you have a connection with Gabriel—and with the whole family, for that matter. They trust you. So we'll use that to our advantage."

Maria looked at him with naked hurt. "How can you be so cold?"

He stared at her, the ice in his soul freezing every opportunity to back away from this precipice. "It's my job, Maria. And the job comes first. It always has."

Thirteen

Maria shut down, her world in ashes. In the cab on the way back to the hotel, she sat without moving, her hands clasped in her lap. Up the elevator, down the hall to Alex's suite. She had to force herself to insert the key card and go inside.

The rooms carried the faint scent of sex and Alex's aftershave mingled with Maria's light perfume. She couldn't even look at the bed. Stoically, she cleared the bathroom of all her paraphernalia. After that, she rounded up her other personal belongings and stuffed them in the tote she had packed with such excitement on Friday evening.

She made it back to her room before breaking

down completely. Sobbing so hard she almost made herself ill, she curled up in a ball on the bed and wondered how she could have thrown herself headlong into such a colossal mistake.

Sleeping with the boss? What a cliché. What a wretched, stupid thing to do. Now, not only was her personal life in ruins, there was a good chance she might have to quit her job. She couldn't face seeing Alex every day at the Department of Commerce. Not knowing what he thought of her.

At the very least, he believed her to be a liar. Far worse than that was the fact he had turned his back on a relationship she thought was incredibly close and special. He'd brushed it aside as if it meant nothing…no more than a blip on the radar.

She'd heard people say that men could have sex without involving their emotions. But she'd never understood exactly what that meant. Now the truth was painfully clear. Alex, either intentionally or as a result of his wide experience with women, had convinced her that what happened in his suite this weekend was the stuff of romantic fantasy.

Fireworks and rainbows and happily-everafters. Realizing she had been so painfully naive was both humiliating and heartbreaking. Alex was willing to pass her off to Gabriel like an unwanted pet. No harm, no foul. Whatever was best for business.

She wanted to hate him for his callousness, and she did. But in the end, Alex was simply being Alex.

Suddenly, she couldn't bear the thought of him knocking on her door to ask something about the proposal or anything else. She called down to the front desk and requested a change of rooms, making up an excuse as to why she wanted to be in the completely opposite wing of the large hotel that encompassed two adjoining buildings connected by a skywalk.

A polite bellman showed up and helped her move her things. It wasn't much of a chore. She had packed light to come to the US. The only extras were a variety of small packages…souvenirs she had purchased for her mother and a few friends.

In the new room, she felt safer, but no less distraught. Changing into the yoga pants and loose cotton top that she had taken with her to Alex's suite, she grimaced. She had envisioned relaxing with him in those simple clothes, maybe watching TV together. Instead, he had kept her naked almost the entire weekend.

Doggedly, she brushed her hair and fixed it in the usual ponytail before donning a baseball cap she wore for jogging to keep the hair out of her eyes. Hopefully, in the casual clothes and the hat no one would recognize her, even if she ran into anyone she knew...which was unlikely.

The members of the delegation were all staying in the other building. The Montoros would either be at the hospital or back in Coral Gables.

She wanted to leave her cell phone behind when she went out. But the tenets of responsibility were too deeply ingrained. This wasn't a vacation. She was here to work. Thus, she had to be available if needed.

For hours, she walked the streets of Miami. South Beach was eclectic and colorful and sophisticated, with its art galleries and restaurants and unique gift shops. Towering high-rises accommodated a wide range of businesses as well as pricey condos. It would be a nice place to live.

At five o'clock, she realized she hadn't eaten

lunch. The fabulous smells emanating from a funky Cuban restaurant drew her inside. Fried plantains and shredded beef over rice filled her stomach, but nothing could fix the aching void in her chest.

She felt more solitary than the time long ago when she had been eight or nine and had to come home from school to an empty house. Those were bleak days. Her mother had worked almost constantly. Maria had learned to do homework on her own, to fix light meals on her own and sometimes even to put herself to bed.

The feeling now was much the same. Fear, dread, desperate loneliness. The only thing different was instead of missing her mother, who was the single touchstone for a child living a chaotic existence, Maria was now a grown woman with a broken heart.

She had told Alex if the weekend was all they had, it would be enough. But she'd been fooling herself. She wanted more. So much more... because despite her best intentions, she had fallen in love with him. It hadn't begun in Miami. She'd been headed in that direction for months, maybe years.

Beneath the hot Florida sun, the truth of her feelings for him had blossomed. For one bright, shining moment, she'd thought he felt it, too. But she had confused sex with caring. Alex was a business associate, the head of the delegation, the boss.

And Maria was nothing but a woman who should have known better.

She was sitting on a bench people-watching when her phone vibrated, signaling a text message.

Where the hell are you?

She could practically feel his anger and frustration.

Your key is at the front desk. Is there anything I need to do for the presentation tomorrow morning? she asked. She wouldn't jump to his bidding without a very good reason.

The document is perfect. I asked where you are.

She waited a long time. Maybe an entire minute. Then grimacing, she composed her answer: I'll see you at nine in the morning.

* * *

Alex stared at his phone in shock, his jaw slack with astonishment. Never in all the years he'd known her had Maria ever behaved like this. She'd been at his beck and call, always willing to work late or to go the extra mile. Time and again he had seen her clean up a shoddy project left behind by someone else. She was driven and intelligent and utterly dependable.

But tonight he didn't even know where she was.

He had gone to her room after dinner, hoping to make things easier between them. But a strange man opened the door when Alex knocked. Alex had backed away with an apology and then examined the number on the door a second time thinking he had made a mistake.

The mistake, however, was far more complex than forgetting a room number. He'd let himself get involved with a coworker. It didn't matter that he wasn't her direct supervisor anymore. He and Maria were in Alma on a critically important mission. Personal relationships were inappropriate at best, for the very reason that they made things complicated.

After his anger had cooled somewhat in the

wake of their confrontation at the hospital, he felt he owed Maria an apology. It wasn't fair to hold her accountable for her feelings if she really was falling for Gabriel Montoro. The man was charismatic, fun-loving and part of a family who had the potential to change Alma for the better over the coming decades.

Grinding his teeth, Alex tossed the phone on the bed and raked both hands through his hair. If he could have come up with even the flimsiest of pretexts to contact Maria again, he would have. But everything was in order for tomorrow's meeting.

Where was she, damn it? He paced the room, trying to ignore the fact that her image appeared everywhere he looked. Like a hologram taunting him with faux reality, she lingered in his bed, on his sofa, in his shower.

Had she gone to Gabriel? Was she with him even now?

Alex forced himself to consider the possibility, confronting it head-on. The pain almost brought him to his knees. How could he let her go? How could he stand by for the good of his country and watch Gabriel Montoro woo her and wed her?

Maria was *his*. He had touched her, made love to her, shuddered in her arms as she pleasured him.

He dropped down on the bed, his head in his hands. How had he made such a mess of his life?

In the hotel conference room the following morning, Alex greeted the members of the committee as they arrived. Maria was conspicuously absent. Once everyone was seated, he passed out the copies of the finished proposal. Excited chatter rose and fell around the table as heads bent to scan the pages he'd had copied at the nearest office-supply store.

Just as Alex stepped behind the portable podium to begin going over the points of the document— section by section—the door opened once again, and Maria slipped into the room with a muttered apology. Her silky blond hair had been tamed into a sleek chignon. She wore a fashionable but relatively conservative navy suit with a pale pink camisole beneath.

Alex's heart stopped entirely and then lurched into motion, his hands damp as they gripped the edge of the wood. "We saved you a seat," he said, trying for friendly humor and failing miserably.

Maria shot him an inscrutable glance and moved toward the opposite end of the table. Normally, she sat near him in case he needed to confer about details or procedure. Today they were as far apart as possible.

Her skin was pale, her eyes underscored with shadows. Had she slept any more than he had?

The men and women around the table barely noticed her arrival. Interest and excitement ran high knowing that today's meeting put them one step closer to officially courting the Montoros.

Alex forced himself to concentrate. This was not the moment to fumble, not with so much at stake. He spoke calmly and clearly, knowing his audience included some of the finest minds Alma had to offer. The Department of State was represented, as were Treasury and Internal Affairs. Combining the business interests of the Montoros with the economy of Alma would require finesse and vision.

It was clear by the end of the first hour that his team was impressed and pleased with the carefully crafted proposal. With the addition of a few footnotes and corrections here and there, the group voted unanimously to approve the document and move on to the next phase…making an official offer to Rafe Montoro IV to return to Alma and accept the throne.

During a short break when Alex had hoped to speak with Maria, his cell phone rang. After a brief conversation, he gathered his papers and reconvened his group. "That was Rafael Montoro on the phone, our potential head of state. He and the entire family had planned to be present tomorrow, as you know, in this very room, to hear what we have to say. But with his aunt in the hospital, they are understandably reluctant to leave her side."

He paused, knowing there was no protocol for this change. "Rafael has asked to come here and receive an unofficial draft, the one you're holding, so that the family might go over it together and discuss it in private. When Isabella recovers, we can then meet officially and make the presentation."

Maria spoke up, her gaze impassive. "Do we have the authority to do that?"

A heated debate ensued, culminating in a conference call to the prime minister back in Alma. Fortunately, after a quick transatlantic conversation, Alex's boss gave the nod. Moments later, Alex made a return call to Rafael.

When that was done, he surveyed the members of the delegation. They had all been cooped up in this room, as pleasant as it was, for hours, and everyone was hungry and tired.

"We'll take a break to eat," he said. "Given Rafael's timetable, we should probably meet back here at three o'clock. Are we all in agreement?"

With nods and muttered assents, the group scattered. Maria, surrounded by three other women, was on her way out before he could stop her. "Wait," he said. The four females turned back to look curiously at him.

He felt his neck get hot. "I need to speak to Maria."

The woman to whom he had made wild, passionate love for hours gave him a cool, regal glance, as if princess to peon. "Right now?"

He stared her down, daring her to ignore him, asserting his authority and knowing that he wasn't playing fair. "Yes."

Maria murmured her apologies to her companions and stepped back into the conference room once they walked away. After closing the door, she set her purse and laptop on the table, crossed her arms and stared at him with barely veiled hostility. "What?"

"Where were you last night?"

Her eyes narrowed. "That is not an appropriate question between business associates."

He had a reputation for being cool under pressure, but, damn, she pushed his buttons. "Were you with Gabriel?"

Her expression was impossible to read. "Are you hoping I'll say yes? So you'll know you have a spy in the enemy camp?"

"Don't be ridiculous."

"Is that why you wanted to talk to me? So you could heap a few more insults on my head?"

If he'd expected any kind of negative response from her, he would have guessed anger. But the mood he picked up on was more akin to sadness. "I wanted to apologize," he said stiffly.

"For what?"

He rounded the table. He'd bet his last euro that she wanted to back away from him, but she maintained her position.

"I shouldn't have connected your relationship with Gabriel to the work of the delegation. Whatever goes on between the two of you is personal and private."

"That's very gracious of you."

The words were innocuous. But they were wrapped in a heavy dose of sarcasm that made him wince.

"I'm trying to make amends," he said.

"And failing miserably. I thought when a man had a one-night stand with a woman, he at least owed her a breakup dinner. Or a Dear Jane note."

"It was two nights." Two insanely erotic, tantalizing nights. Even now, the memory made him hard.

"I won't quibble over the details, Alex. All I ask is that next time you want to scratch a sexual itch, you find someone who doesn't mind being shoved aside when your job takes precedence."

"That's not what happened."

"What would *you* call it?" she asked.

"You and I have worked together a long time. There was bound to be an undercurrent of sexual interest. But I was wrong to pursue it, given the circumstances."

"You act as if it was all your idea. I was in the bed, too. So let's call it a dual mistake."

As they exchanged barbs, he moved closer. Now, he snagged one of her hands in his and put his thumb over the pulse point on her wrist. "I'm asking you to forgive me," he said huskily. It was only now dawning on him that physical proximity to the woman who turned him inside out might not be the best idea.

She didn't struggle or try to free herself, though his hold was loose. Because they stood so closely together, she was forced to tip back her head to look up at him. "Forgive you for what?"

Blue-green eyes that were usually guileless and clear were veiled today, the emotions carefully blanked out.

"Stubborn, frustrating woman." His lips hovered over hers, his body straining to get closer. He maintained a safe distance between them, but it cost him.

One kiss. That's all he needed. An apology kiss. That made sense, didn't it? For one quivering, tense second, he knew it was going to happen. He felt it inside his gut. Every cell in his body cried out for him to ignore reason and reality and to take what he wanted.

Maria was frozen in place, her arms still crossed at her waist. The brittle edge of her anger had softened. He was sure of it. "I really am sorry," he muttered. "For everything."

His lips brushed hers with a spark of contact electricity. *Holy hell.*

The jolt rocked him. "Say something, Maria."

Two slender feminine hands struck his shoulders and shoved hard, catching him off guard, causing him to lose his balance and fall into the nearest chair.

Before he could recover, she was gone.

Fourteen

Maria caught up with her lunch companions at the restaurant downstairs. She was coldly furious, but she wallowed in the icy, cleansing emotion. For the moment, it cauterized the jagged edges of her broken heart. Alex Ramon was an imbecile.

He thought he could manipulate her and use her and get away with his double-talk, avoiding a single consequence to his oh-so-perfect image. Maybe other women had been willing to accept his Dr. Jekyll and Mr. Hyde routine, but not this one.

And he still didn't believe her about Gabriel.

It took all the acting skills she could muster, but

she engaged in the conversation among her colleagues without giving a hint at the turmoil that
rocked her. She prayed that the Montoros would
make their decision quickly, one way or another.
All Maria wanted to do was go home.

After lunch she made a quick trip to her room
to drop off her laptop, brush her teeth and freshen
her lipstick. An official visit between Rafe Montoro and the delegation as a whole required a
certain degree of formality. She wanted to look
her best.

Lingering deliberately until the last possible
moment, she made her way back to the conference room and took her original seat. The fur-
niture had been rearranged to accommodate a
head table. Someone from the hotel had brought
in a small vase of fresh flowers.

The tension in the room was palpable.

Her arrogant lover spotted her the moment she
walked in, but though he gave her a steady look,
he did nothing to summon her attention. Once
everyone from Alma was seated, the group fell
silent.

Alex stepped into the hallway and returned
with Rafael. But the king-to-be was not alone.

Gabriel was with him. That came as no surprise to Maria. The brothers were close.

The two Montoros were dressed formally in dark suits and ties. Even Gabriel, rascal that he was, maintained his composure. Alex took a visible breath. "Ladies and gentlemen. May I present Rafael Montoro, IV, and his brother, Gabriel." Facing the siblings, he executed a half bow. "On behalf of the nation of Alma, we welcome both of you this afternoon and look forward to hearing what you have to say."

Alex stepped aside and offered Rafe the podium.

The eldest of this younger Montoro generation spoke pleasantly and confidently. As CEO of Montoro Enterprises, he was accustomed to a leadership role, so he showed no signs of being nervous or intimidated by the fact that an entire roomful of people wanted to make him a king.

Rafael was tall, a couple of inches over six feet. His dark brown hair, cut very short, suited his air of command.

When he was done with his brief, prepared remarks, he fielded questions. Through it all, Gabriel remained quiet but watchful, as if he were trying to assess the character of each member of the delegation.

Other than a couple of polite inquiries, no one introduced any kind of controversial topics. There would be time enough for that later.

Toward the end of the hour, when a note of awkward anticipation entered the mix, Gabriel and Maria exchanged rueful glances. This was a touchy situation, however you looked at it.

Rafael nodded briefly to his audience, for a split second betraying the first hint of agitation Maria had seen from him. "I hope you'll understand that we need to get back to the hospital," he said. "My family and I will read through this proposal and give it our utmost consideration."

He paused. "I am well aware that each of you has gone above and beyond the expectations of your job descriptions. From what Mr. Ramon has told me, you have given your time and talents to this endeavor with varying degrees of personal sacrifice. I am honored by this proposal, and I will weigh the ramifications as honestly as I know how. Thank you."

Quiet applause greeted his last words. The group rose as one, everybody eager to say a word of greeting to the man who might one day reign as their monarch. During the hubbub, Gabriel scooted around the room in Maria's direction. His smile was strained. "This bunch is making me claustrophobic," he said. "Will you come with me for a minute?"

"Of course." He seemed oblivious to Alex's displeasure.

They found an empty meeting space across the hall, much smaller than the one they'd escaped, and slipped inside to hide out in the back corner.

Gabriel leaned against the wall and rubbed his face. "I wish I still smoked," he groaned.

"You smoked?" Maria asked with a frown.

His charming grin radiated only half its usual voltage. "For about eight months the year I turned sixteen. When my father found out, he hit the ceiling. He and Rafe took me out on a sailboat and made me smoke two entire packs during one afternoon…in rough seas, I might add. I spent the next hour hanging over the rail barfing my guts out. That was the last day I ever wanted a cigarette. Until now."

She touched his arm. "You've got a lot going on in your family. I know it's hard. How's Isabella?"

"Holding her own. We were all afraid this was it, but she's a tough old bird." He rolled his shoulders. "The timing sucks, though. We need to get the proposal mess settled one way or another."

"How is Rafe leaning? You can trust me. I won't say a word to anyone."

"I wish I knew. I thought Isabella's health crisis would tip the scales, but she made it clear to us yesterday afternoon that she only wants the family to say yes to the proposal if we can do it with unanimity and one hundred percent enthusiasm."

"That sounds like an impossible goal."

"Yeah. So I haven't the slightest idea how this is going to turn out."

"I wish there was something I could do to make it easier."

"That's sweet of you. You're a very nice lady." He flicked her updo. "Was it my imagination, or were things tense between you and Alex at the hospital? I got the impression he'd like to punch me. Has my charade worked? Does he think he'll have to battle me to win you back?"

She blushed. "Oh, that was nothing. We had a difference of opinion about something. It's not important."

Gabriel bent his head and locked eyes with her, his trademark grin wider than it had been so far today. "I have good instincts when it comes to romance. I think the two of you are an item."

"Did we trip and fall into a fifties movie? Don't make me laugh. Alex Ramon is a stuffed shirt. A workaholic. A soulless bureaucrat."

The fact that her voice broke on the last syllable was a dead giveaway. She turned her back on Gabriel, mortified that she was making a scene.

He curled an arm around her shoulders. "You want me to beat him up for you?"

She wiped her face with the back of her hand. "Would you?"

They both laughed, and she felt better, despite the fact that the man she loved was still a jerk.

A cold, rigid voice broke them apart. "Excuse me. I didn't know I was interrupting."

Gabriel whirled around, striding forward to clap Alex on the shoulder. "Not at all. Maria was just commiserating with me about my family's multiple soap-opera-ish woes."

When Alex continued to resemble a silent, stony-faced executioner, Gabriel shook his head.

"You've got the wrong end of the stick, Ramon. I don't poach on another man's preserves."

Maria frowned. "What does that mean?"

Gabriel shot her a look over his shoulder. "It means that you and I are buddies, amigos, compadres. But what we are *not* is an item."

His humor fell flat all the way around.

Alex nodded stiffly. "I didn't mean any disrespect."

Gabriel rolled his eyes. "I'm not a prince yet. I don't need bowing and scraping from you." He held out his hand. "Are we good, man?"

Alex nodded, the harsh lines in his face relaxing. "We're good. Thanks for coming today. I think your brother is waiting for you."

"No problem. You've done a good job leading this delegation, Alex. Our family is grateful for your sensitivity and your diplomacy. And, by the by, I want you to call me Gabriel."

"I suppose in the interim it would be okay."

"It will *always* be okay," Gabriel said firmly. "Even if Rafe accepts this king-of-Alma gig, I guarantee he'll only tolerate so much pomp and circumstance. You and Maria have made our family feel as if our wishes and opinions are valid. That goes a long way in the negotiating process. We appreciate it."

Alex nodded. "I'm glad you feel that way."

Gabriel, now by the door, sketched a wave at Maria. "I've got to run, sweet thing. See you soon."

Suddenly the party of three became two.

Maria shifted from one foot to the other. Alex stood between her and an escape route. "Is everyone else gone?" she asked.

He nodded. "Yes."

"Are you pleased with how today turned out?"

Alex weighed his answer. "Not entirely."

"What's wrong? Did Rafe say something? Are they trying to tell you this is going nowhere?"

Alex held up his hands. "Whoa. Slow down the train. I wasn't talking about anything that happened in an official capacity. You asked me if I was pleased with how today turned out, and I said no…because things are at an impasse between you and me."

"Not my fault." Her glare melted his certainty that he could persuade her to see reason.

"I've already apologized," he said. "Can't we move on?"

Memories of her in his bed tangled with the reality of Maria standing in front of him. She was neat and feminine and so damned beautiful in her trendy suit. But her clothing reminded him that they were colleagues first and lovers second… not an order he wanted, but a necessity given the situation with the Montoros.

Her lips trembled. "You don't even get it, do you? I'm not upset because you kicked me out of your bed. I'm furious and astounded that you didn't believe *me* when I told you nothing was going on with Gabriel. Yet when *he* told you the exact same thing, suddenly you take it as fact."

Alex realized he'd screwed up royally. The pun didn't even register as funny. "Perhaps we should take a couple of steps backward and start over." He was aiming for calm and conciliatory. Maria didn't seem impressed.

She walked across the room and went toe-to-toe with him. "There's nothing to start over *with*. We're not anything to each other, Alex. Just a man and a woman who happen to work together."

Deliberately, she elbowed him aside and made for the door.

His temper snapped and flared. "Not so fast."

Dragging her against his chest, he took her chin in his hand and tilted it upward so he could reach her gorgeous, argumentative lips. Instead of angry mastery, he clamped down on his aggravation and gave her gentleness, trying every way he knew how to convey his regret that he had made such a mess of things.

But it was a lost cause. Her body was stiff in his embrace...her lips cold and unresponsive. Reluctantly, he released her. A block of ice settled in the spot where his stomach had been.

She stared at him, her gaze neither stormy nor sweet. Instead, she was indifferent. "Next time you do that, Mr. Ramon, I'll report you for sexual harassment. Good day."

When she walked out on him, Alex was stunned.

He stood in the small empty room for a full five minutes, trying to analyze where he'd gone wrong. All his life he'd been an overachiever. Top of his class in every school he'd ever attended. His father's favorite. A goal-oriented, don't-give-up, type A, hardworking guy who went after whatever he wanted and got it.

Money had never been an issue. His parents

had spoiled him, but he had repaid their gener-osity by consistently making them proud of him. He'd never yearned and ached for something he couldn't have, had never faced real, honest-to-God disappointment and failure.

This was a hell of a moment to learn an unpleas-ant life lesson. Apparently he wasn't infallible after all. There was at least a fifty-fifty chance that the Montoros were going to decline the re-quest to reclaim the monarchy. Which meant that Alex and the delegation would have wasted weeks and months of planning and positioning.

Going home to Alma empty-handed, with the proposal unsigned, would not only be a personal defeat, it would constitute an embarrassing mis-step in Alex's career. People had depended on him. His *country* had entrusted him with a mis-sion of incalculable importance.

Forcing himself to take a painful look at his be-havior this past weekend was mildly reassuring. Even though he had let his personal life intrude during a time he should have been concentrating on the Montoros, he honestly didn't think mak-ing love to Maria had been any kind of derelic-tion of duty.

His worst sin lay in allowing her to believe that he didn't respect or value her as a person and woman.

That had never been his intention, but looking at the situation from her point of view, he could now see how badly he had bungled things. She was hurt that he thought she was a liar. Nothing could be further from the truth. But when she told him nothing was going on with her and Gabriel, he'd assumed she simply didn't recognize the other man's interest.

The truth was, Alex couldn't imagine any red-blooded male being immune to Maria's charms.

When he had handed her his room key and asked her to remove her things, he'd been operating from hurt and jealousy and anger. Though he'd told himself it was the right thing to do because of his position as head of the delegation, the truth was, he'd been reeling from seeing her in the garden with Gabriel.

Alex had never cared enough about any woman to be affected one way or another if the female in question found someone else. His work had always been at the forefront of his priority list.

Satisfying his physical needs had come second. He liked sex as much as the next guy and enjoyed women and their soft bodies and interesting minds.

But not once in his life had he ever experienced this gnawing feeling of emptiness and loss.

Hubris brought down many a man. Recognizing his failings had certainly chastened and humbled Alex. Now he faced a double-barrel shotgun ready to destroy much of his life. If this had happened six months ago, he would have been obsessing over how he could save face and salvage his career.

At this moment, however, he didn't give a damn about losing his reputation or his job or anything else that might be part of the Montoro fallout.

His only regret was that he had screwed up the one exquisitely wonderful, warm and perfect relationship he'd ever experienced. He had lost Maria's good regard, her friendship and any prospect of having her in his bed.

And there was a dollop of bitter gall on top of this mountainous fiasco. He knew one truth beyond any shadow of doubt. He was in love with Maria Ferro.

* * *

Maria didn't know what to do. She was not an indecisive person, but she felt as if the walls had caved in on her.

Her first impulse was to call the airline to see about changing her ticket. But when she tried, the cost was ridiculous, and even then, she couldn't get a seat until the following week because of a baggage handler strike.

The impulse to run was overpowering. She didn't want to face Alex and would try to avoid him for as long as possible. When they were eventually together again, would he be able to read heartbreak in her face? Would he guess that she was in love with him?

When flying home early didn't work, she decided it was for the best. To leave without saying goodbye to the Montoros would be terribly rude, particularly with Isabella in the hospital.

Two days later, Maria sat in a coffee shop a few blocks from the hotel and scrolled through emails halfheartedly. The past forty-eight hours had dragged by. The only news of note was that Isabella had improved dramatically and would be returning home. Her diagnosis, of course, was still terminal, but doctors gave her an open-ended amount of time to live, so everyone involved was thankful.

While all that was happening, Maria had read books, walked on the beach and even taken a bus tour of the city. Anything to pass the time.

Waiting was excruciating. She could only imagine how Alex must feel. Today was even worse, and it wasn't yet noon. She and her mom chatted online for a bit. Hearing about events back in Alma seemed strange…as if the world should have stopped while Maria was in Miami.

Finally, just as she was ordering a sandwich for her lunch, a text came through. From Gabriel.

Don't say a word to anyone, but we're close!

Her heart stopped. Immediately, she wanted to call Alex, but of course, she couldn't. She answered quickly.

Will there be a monarchy?

It looks that way. God help us…

She had a feeling Gabriel meant those last three words literally. The task set forth before Rafael was enormous, but the entire family would be affected in so many ways.

Does Isabella know? she texted.

Not yet. Rafe and Dad want to make sure all the *t*'s are crossed and *i*'s dotted.

Makes sense.

If this all comes to pass, big party planned. Other news for the Montoros to announce.

Tell me. Tell me.

My lips are sealed.

She could almost see his smirk.

Thanks for the heads-up.

You bet. See you soon.

Maria paid for her sandwich and sat down to eat it, but she had lost her appetite. If she and Alex hadn't argued, Alex would probably have included her in all of this last-minute hush-hush negotiation. As it was, she'd been left out in the cold. She was surprised at how much that hurt.

Her phone lay on the table. Surely Alex would tell her when it happened. Or maybe things had fallen apart. She shoved her half-eaten lunch aside and bit her fingernail, a bad habit she'd given up in high school.

It was thirty-seven minutes from Gabriel's text until the next time her phone dinged quietly. This time the message on the screen was from Alex. It was simple and to the point.

We have a king!

Tears sprang to her eyes. She knew exactly how Alex would look right now. Jubilant. Relieved. Incredibly handsome.

He had not texted her privately. One by one, the replies came in until it became clear he had included the entire delegation in a group message. Maria was one of the crowd.

Knowing she had to say something or risk seeming oddly silent to her colleagues, she bit her lip and slowly composed her answer.

A great day for Alma. I am proud to have worked alongside all of you.

Then she shut off her phone. There was only the minutest of chances that Alex would call her, but she couldn't take a chance. Hearing his voice would tear her apart.

Grabbing up her things and her tote bag, she tossed the remains of her lunch in the trash and set out to walk the streets of Miami. Maybe she could outrun her demons. And maybe the moon was made of green cheese.

Her life had changed. It would change even more back in Alma. She had some big decisions to make.

Fifteen

Alex couldn't remember the last time he'd been this tired or this satisfied. Or this frustrated. He barely knew what to think from one moment to the next.

When Rafe Montoro rang to say he was signing the document but with a few caveats, a firestorm of phone calls had ensued. The prime minister had to be roused from his bed back in Alma. The time difference would make the next few days challenging as the two parties resolved minor differences.

As a show of good faith, Rafael IV planned to make a quick trip to Alma very soon to sign a new agreement between Montoro Enterprises and a major refinery in Alma to ship oil to the US.

After the long days and weeks of waiting and wondering, suddenly it was all happening very quickly.

Alex tried Maria's phone three separate times, but the calls went straight to voice mail. Where the hell was she? With Gabriel? Even if nothing romantic was going on between the two of them, it was clear to Alex that Gabriel and Maria were becoming very good friends.

Alex had thought, once upon a time, that *he* and Maria were close. But now she had deliberately put distance between them. Knowing that the situation was his own fault didn't help.

For the remainder of the day until late in the night he fielded communications between Alma and the soon-to-be royal family. Decisions had to be made about the timing of public announcements. In the interests of good business, it was important to protect the Montoros' image here in the States as well as abroad.

The stock market didn't like change or uncertainty, and Montoro Enterprises was a publicly traded company. All the kinks needed to be ironed out before revealing this extraordinary news.

For the next seventy-two hours, Alex worked pretty much nonstop, existing on four to five hours of sleep a night. Though he and Maria communicated via text and email, when they labored side by side at the table, there was always someone else in the room.

Alex could have forced the issue, demanding that they meet in private. But he had done enough damage already. So he chose to bide his time.

The truth was, he didn't have the luxury of worrying about his personal life at a time like this. All of his attention had to be focused on Alma and the Montoros and the changes to come.

But when he finally fell into bed during the wee hours of the morning, he lay in the darkness remembering the feel of Maria's body pressed up against his and imagining he could still detect the scent of her perfume on his pillow.

Maria smoothed the skirt of her fire-engine-red gown and wondered if she had made a mistake. Looking in the bathroom mirror, she tugged at the bodice, hoping to cover at least half an inch more cleavage. Her breasts were modest in size, but with the cut of the fabric and the sewn-in boning, everything she had was up and out on display.

When the news leaked that the Montoros were accepting Alma's proposal, all heck had broken loose. Maria had spent long hours with her laptop preparing press releases in a variety of formats. Some for Alma, others for the local Miami market, and still more for the entire United States and the rest of the world.

A political event of this magnitude had repercussions that would echo for years to come. It was exciting and challenging to be part of the process. All her education and training and hard work had led to this pivotal moment. She should be proud. And she was.

But all the job satisfaction in the world did little to mend a broken heart, especially in light of the knowledge that she would most likely have to look for other work when she went home.

Already, she realized that she couldn't be in the same building as Alex and pretend that she didn't care. She wasn't the first woman to be mistaken about a man, and she wouldn't be the last.

But the hurt ran deep.

What she needed to do in the meantime was to compartmentalize. Personal feelings—locked away. Fun-and-games Maria—out to play. Tonight's party at the Montoro compound in Coral Gables was likely to be the glitziest, most glamorous affair she'd ever attended. To hell with Alex Ramon and his arrogant judgmental attitude. Maria was going to enjoy herself.

In between frantic work sessions, she had slipped away yesterday afternoon and found a boutique at one of the nearby hotels that showcased the work of a local designer. Although of runway quality, the woman's designs were still relatively unknown and the prices were not astronomical.

In addition to the pale aqua dress she wore at the opening reception, Maria had brought with her from Alma two easy-to-pack outfits for formal occasions that might arise, but neither was particularly exciting. So when she had spotted this sexy red number, she'd had to try it on. Even the saleslady had been visibly impressed. The color was perfect for Maria's skin and hair.

The splendid creation made her feel like a princess. Which was not a bad thing on an evening when a monarchy was about to be reborn.

She eyed the tiny straps and fitted waist. Though she couldn't see the entire silhouette, she ran her hands down her hips, feeling the way the silk hugged her curves. Below the knees it fanned out in a mermaidlike froth of tulle and satin.

Maybe she would meet a handsome local who would sweep her off her feet. Maybe they would dance until dawn.

It was a nice image, but even as she turned away from her reflection, she had to blink back tears. She would not cry for Alex Ramon. Not tonight. Tonight was a time for celebration.

Maria was in the lobby, bags packed, at five o'clock. Bella had insisted on coming to pick her up in a limo. The entire delegation, as a courtesy, had been offered accommodations in the various guest villas at the Montoros' Coral Gables estate for the weekend.

Several cars were being dispatched to the hotel to ferry Alma's guests of honor to the soiree. Fortunately, Maria didn't have to worry about an uncomfortable encounter with Alex.

Bella's eyebrows went up when she walked in and saw Maria. "You look fantastic."

"Thank you," Maria said. "You're good for my ego." As the driver stowed Maria's bags, Bella and Maria settled on opposite sides of the wide seat and fastened their seat belts.

Bella frowned. "Don't take this as a criticism, but you look like you've been crying."

Her matter-of-fact assessment sent Maria scrambling for the small, mirrored compact in her evening purse. "Do I?"

As she scanned her face hurriedly, Bella chuckled. "That was just a test. If you'd told me you hadn't been crying, I'd have known you were okay. But I can see it in your eyes. You and Alex haven't made up, have you? Gabriel told me what's going on."

Maria gave her a sour look. "Not funny. And there's nothing to make up. Alex and I are fine."

"Never kid a kidder." Bella reached into the small refrigerator and poured a glass of champagne, handing it to her with a sympathetic smile.

"Chin up. He may take one look at you in that dress and keel over at your feet..."

Unfortunately, Bella's blithe pronouncement was way off the mark. When Maria first spotted Alex, he was deep in conversation with a local news anchorwoman who looked far more interested in her interviewee than in the Montoro story.

Although Alex spared a brief glance in Maria's direction, his gaze didn't linger. So much for the red dress.

Instead of bemoaning something she couldn't change, she chose to soak up the splendor of the evening. The backdrop for tonight's festivities exhibited all the glamour and drama of a movie set. Lush lawns lay like green velvet, punctuated with every manner of tropical bush and flower amid towering palm trees.

White tents, strung with lights that would eventually twinkle against the night sky, provided shelter in case of inclement weather, but so far, the clouds only served to accentuate what would be a dramatic sunset.

Caterers were hard at work setting out china and crystal and, most impressive of all, heavy silver utensils bearing the Montoro crest. The precious metal dated back to the eighteenth century and had been hidden away in a root cellar by a faithful servant when the Montoro ancestors fled for their lives.

Most recently it had been on display in a museum in Alma but, under Alex's directions, had been flown across the ocean for tonight's party. Maria gave a moment's pause to wonder how safe it was to actually use such priceless artifacts, but security was heavy and visible.

Everyone had been required to enter through a special gate where professional teams of men and women used hand wands and other means to ensure that only invited guests were allowed in.

Bella glanced at her watch. "I hate to abandon you, but I promised my father I'd take care of a few things."

Maria smiled, shooing her away. "I'm fine. Go. I may hide out in my room for a bit if you'll tell me where I'm staying." The limo driver had absconded with her luggage.

Maria's smile was rueful. "I wasn't in charge of the lodging assignments. The housekeeper put you and Alex in the same villa you had before."

Maria gaped. "Please tell me you're joking."

"Sorry." She seemed genuinely apologetic. "Every bed is taken."

"Never mind then," Maria said grumpily, her panic barely under control. "I'll make myself useful somewhere."

Bella walked away, leaving Maria to wander the grounds in limbo until the main event started. Did Alex already know they were sharing a villa? Was he angry about it? Was that why he had barely looked at her when she arrived?

If she had imagined being bored during the wait, nothing could have been further from the truth. Perching on a fabric-covered chair in an out-of-the-way corner, she had a perfect view of the guests as they arrived. It was almost like the red carpet at the Oscars.

Since she wasn't from Miami, or even an American, many of the faces were not recognizable to her. But it was easy to spot the ones who graced the covers of the tabloids. Rock legends and rappers. Television personalities. Stars of stage and screen. The Montoros were infinitely more well-connected than she had realized.

At the far end of the lawn, with the ocean as

an azure background, a small stage had been erected along with a high-tech sound system. At seven o'clock, the evening was to kick off with formalities. After that, on to dinner and dancing.

She had waved at Gabriel from a distance, but he had two gorgeous women with him, one on each arm, so she didn't intrude.

By the time the dignitaries took the stage, Maria was a nervous wreck. She wanted to give Alex a word of encouragement, but with the discord between the two of them, it was probably best to keep her distance. Personal feelings had to make way for the important business at hand.

She wished desperately that she were one of the carefree partygoers with nothing but pleasure on her mind. The festive crowd mingled and moved like a vibrant, colorful flock of birds, the men's black-tie apparel providing a backdrop for the female plumage.

A hush fell as Rafael Montoro III, his three children and Alex ascended the shallow steps and took their seats. Only the eldest member of the group remained standing. He approached the podium and looked out over the sea of faces, his expression full of emotion.

He cleared his throat. "It is my great pleasure to welcome each of you into the heart of the Montoro family this evening. We are proud citizens of the United States of America, and Florida has been our home and our sanctuary. Nothing will ever take away that bond. But life is full of surprises, and as you all understand, the only constant is change."

He paused as laughter greeted his remarks.

"For any of you who do not know me," he said, "I am Rafael Montoro III. On the podium with me tonight are my three children—Rafael IV, Gabriel and Bella. We look forward to chatting with as many of you as possible during this wonderful evening. There is much to celebrate. I am proud to say that as of this week, Montoro Enterprises has officially been listed in the Fortune 500 for the very first time."

This time the response was wild and loud, punctuated with cheering and high fives.

He waited, smiling, for the hubbub to die down. "Now I would like to introduce Mr. Alex Ramon, deputy prime minister of commerce for Alma, and also the leader of the delegation from that country."

Alex and Rafael exchanged a half handshake, half embrace before the older man sat down. When Alex adjusted the microphone to accommodate his greater height, Maria's palms were as damp as if she were standing there beside him.

But when he spoke, his words resonated with such passion and conviction and sheer charisma, she forgot for a moment that he had shared life's most intimate act with her. Instead, she listened intently, filled with pride and admiration for the man who had accomplished so much.

After a brief explanatory statement, Alex smiled and asked Rafe to join him. "It is my great honor and privilege to present to you the next king of the nation of Alma, Rafael Montoro IV."

Rafe, perhaps unnerved by the import of the moment, nodded, his features tense. But his shoulders relaxed somewhat when Alex indicated that he should say something.

"It's early days yet," Rafe finally said, "and I am deeply cognizant of the honor bestowed upon me by the people of Alma. But I want you to know that I take this commitment very seriously, and I will do everything in my power to ensure this new relationship brings progress and benefit to the people who are entrusting me with their leadership."

This time, the applause had a different tone. Everyone in earshot had an inkling of what Rafael faced. It was not an easy thing to rule, and they offered him their respect along with their congratulations.

To Maria's surprise, Rafael sat down, and Alex once again took the podium. "I would be remiss tonight if I did not recognize each member of the official delegation from Alma. You'll find their names printed in your programs. I hope you will take the time to greet them this evening and express your appreciation for their hard work and dedication to the idea of restoring Alma's monarchy."

He stopped talking abruptly, and, for a split second, Maria felt as if he were staring straight at her. "The thing is," he said, the words contemplative, "politics and business negotiations encompass far more than dry statistics and formal agreements. In the end, it's all about relationships. About people. About trust and integrity. One member of our group seems to understand that truth at a most basic level, and I am not sure we would be standing here tonight were it not for the wise counsel and collaborative efforts of the lovely lady in the red dress, Ms. Maria Ferro. Thank you, Maria, for all you have done to build bridges and bring consensus to the table."

She never heard the applause this time. Her heart was beating too loudly in her ears to take in anything else. People around her shook her hand and kissed her cheek and offered words of congratulations. It was all a blur.

Suddenly, Alex was at her side, looking darkly handsome and so very dear. His firm jaw and classic features made him stand out, even in an assembly of very good-looking men.

He didn't touch her. But the searing look he gave her made her shiver. "I nearly swallowed my tongue when you walked into my line of sight earlier," he muttered, the words husky. "You and that dress should be an illegal combination."

"Did you mean what you said?" she asked. "Or did the delegation tell you to spout all that?"

"God, sweetheart. I really screwed up, didn't I? Of *course* I meant it. Every word."

It was gratifying to know that he valued her

work, but his compliments didn't erase the fact that he didn't trust her.

Suddenly, she became aware that several people were standing close enough to take interested note of what they were saying.

Alex took her arm, his fingers warm and strong on her bare skin. "Let's get out of here."

She eluded his hold. "No. I don't have anything to say to you. You've never believed me when it comes to Gabriel, and that hurts."

"I do believe you," he said urgently. "But I thought you were fooling yourself about *his* feelings. Turns out I was dead wrong. About everything."

"Gabriel and I are friends."

"I know that now. I've been a total ass. And I'm sorry. I was jealous and stupid. I don't deserve it, but I'm asking you to forgive me."

She gaped in surprise at his unequivocal about-face. Alex took advantage of her shock to hurry her along.

They made it as far as the last tent before she dug in her heels. *"Alex,"* she said urgently. "I forgive you. I really do. But this is your night. This is Alma's night. Everything you've dreamed of and worked for the last eighteen months. You can't walk out on the party."

He kissed her softly, lingering long enough to make her breath catch and her knees go weak. "Watch me, my love."

Grabbing an empty golf cart, he pulled her onto the seat beside him and started the motor. She wasn't sure she'd have been able to find her way through the maze of paths, but Alex took them straight to the small, charming villa where they had stayed on their first visit to Coral Gables.

When he removed his foot from the pedal, the cart rolled to a stop, and Maria felt her belly quiver. She tried to speak, but her throat was so dry the words stuck there unvoiced.

Perhaps Alex sensed her agitation, or perhaps he was simply in a hurry. Either way, he took her by surprise when he scooped her up and carried her around to the front door. The villa wasn't locked. They found the key inside on a table with a note of greeting from their hosts, a basket of fruit and an arrangement of fresh flowers.

Alex secured the door with one hand, not even breathing hard.

Finally, she found the words she wanted to say. "Thank you."

He frowned. "For what?"

She touched his chin. A tiny nick on the left side of his jaw told her his late-day shave had been hurried. "For saying all those nice things. And for groveling so sweetly."

Finally, a note of humor lightened his face. "If you think *that* was nice, you ain't seen nothin' yet."

He bypassed the luxurious living room and went straight down the hall, only hesitating between the two bedrooms. "Your place or mine?"

Maria decided it was about time to rein in all that assured masculinity. "Aren't you assuming a lot, Mr. Ramon?"

He kicked open the door to the room that had been Maria's on their last visit. Dropping her on the mattress, he took her small purse from her nerveless fingers and tossed it aside. Coming down beside her, he leaned on one elbow, his expression sober. "I was an ass and an idiot, but I adore you, Maria. My life means nothing if you aren't in it. Say you love me. Say you forgive me. Marry me and give me babies."

The arrogance was still there. Nothing but demands. Her heart swelled anyway. "You may be a diplomat, but you're terrible at groveling."

He slid off the bed and knelt on the rug, his dark eyes sober. Reaching out, he took her hand in his. "We got off to a rocky start. I wish I could have wooed you in private, at our leisure, not in the midst of a ticking political time bomb. You deserve so much better."

"I *like* working with you," she said softly, curling her fingers with his.

She saw his throat work when he swallowed. "My only excuse is that it took me by surprise."

"*What* did?"

"The fact that I'm in love with you."

She stopped breathing for at least five seconds. "You really love me?"

"Isn't that what I've been saying?" His masculine indignation made her smile.

"Somehow, when you distill it to those three words, it seems more real. I love you, too, Alex." She sat up and leaned forward, curling a hand behind his head to kiss him. "I think I probably have for a long time."

"If you like real," he muttered, "you're going to like what I've got planned next."

He ripped off his tux jacket and jerked at his shirt, sending studs flying. Her pulse sped up and stuttered. "Shall I help?"

"No. Come here."

Poor man. He couldn't help himself. He was accustomed to being in charge. But they could work on that.

She shimmied off the bed and stood in front of him. Though he was taller, her heels put them eye-to-eye. Tracing a finger from one side of his collarbone to the other, she sighed. His hard, broad, warm chest was a thing of beauty. "I'm kind of sorry we didn't stay," she murmured, kissing the spot where a pulse beat in his neck.

His hands fisted at his sides. "Why is that?" The words were little more than a croak. Between them, his erection tented the front of his trousers.

Curling her arms around his neck, she rested her cheek on his shoulder. "I had dreams of dancing with you."

"Hold that thought," he said.

He released her and searched his jacket until he came up with his phone. Clicking icons as he concentrated, he found what he wanted. Moments later a classic love song began playing softly.

"Oh, Alex…"

He took her in his arms and teased gently. "Oh, Maria."

"I'm still not sure how this is going to work back at home," she fretted. "People will talk."

"The only thing people will say is how smart I am to have snagged you before some other guy found you first."

His hand on the bare skin of her back was firm and hot. "Have I told you how much I love this dress?"

"That's a lot of the *L* word floating around from a man who has a reputation for being buttoned up."

He stepped back and held out his arms, a sexy grin tilting the corners of his mouth. "Does *this* look like I'm buttoned up?"

"Good point." She wrapped her arms around his waist this time, swaying to the romantic melody.

Alex dipped her without warning. "Are you attached to this dress?" he asked, lifting her upright again.

Dark color slashed his cheekbones. His eyes glittered with emotions she recognized. Hunger. Need. Desperation. It might as well have been years since they had made love, so urgent was the wave of yearning that pulsed between them.

She licked her lips. "It cost a lot of money. I was going to wear it all evening."

"I'll be careful with it then," he muttered, lowering her zipper before she could do more than squeak. "And the night's still young. We might make it back to the party…"

"Fair enough." He was lying, and she didn't even care.

Slipping the narrow straps of her red fit-for-a-princess gown down her arms, he groaned when he realized she wasn't wearing a bra. Her nipples tightened as he stared at her breasts.

"I want you."

It seemed as if he had been reduced to caveman syllables, but she understood entirely.

Holding his hand as she stepped out of her bikini undies, she faced him wearing nothing but stilettos and a tentative smile. "I want you, too. All these years we've known each other I admired you, but it took me a while to realize that my feelings went way beyond that. You're a difficult man to resist."

"Then don't even try, sweetheart."

He dragged her up against him until nothing separated them but the fabric of his tux pants. The feeling was exquisite. But she had a feeling it could be even better.

Her fingers stroked his lower back. "I need you naked. Hurry."

"Whatever the lady wants."

Alex pulled away and managed the task with clumsy speed and harsh breathing.

When he was done, he tumbled them both onto the mattress, making her laugh. "I like this wild and crazy Alex," she said.

He reached for his pants that he'd tossed on the corner of the mattress. Extracting a small box, he handed it to her. "Marry me, Maria. Please."

The raw, almost awkward proposal caught her off guard and sent her heart spinning. The ring was gorgeous, a single solitaire, large enough to signal ships at sea. "It's beautiful."

He slipped it on her finger. "That's not an answer."

"Yes," she muttered, emotion making it difficult to speak. "Yes, Alex."

He stroked her from throat to belly, his warm, slightly rough touch igniting sparks everywhere he went. "Don't ever leave me again," he muttered, his expression darkly serious.

His intensity humbled her. She brushed her thumb across his lower lip. "I won't. But you know we'll still fight once in a while. We're both bullheaded."

He moved over her and into her with firm, gentle possession that made her lift against him, sighing, her legs wrapped around his waist.

Alex rested his forehead on hers. "Fighting is okay. As long as we call a truce every night."

She bit her lip when his thrust hit a certain spot. The physical sensation was second only to emotional bliss. The fact that he was here with her in this bed spoke volumes. Barely a quarter mile away, the high point of his professional career played out among the rich and famous. But Alex had made his choice.

His love humbled and elated her.

When the moment of no return neared, rational thought gave way to sensation. Heat. Tenderness. Skin to skin. Heart to heart. Damp skin to damp skin.

Her body jerked as the climax hit, sending her tumbling amid the sparks. Alex held her tightly.

His end came moments later, a raw groan of stunned pleasure.

Lying together in a tangle of arms and legs, they breathed raggedly.

As she ran her toe up the back of his calf, she grumbled. "We can do this all night, I swear. But they need you at the party, Alex. Honestly, they do."

A mighty sigh rolled through his chest. "I know."

"The sooner we get dressed, the sooner we can come back here."

"A bribe, Maria?"

"Did it work?"

He bit the side of her neck. "Yes, damn it."

She smiled, even though he couldn't see it. "I love you, Mr. Ramon."

Alex rolled out of bed and picked up her red dress, his scowl dark as he eyed her naked body. "Put this back on before I change my mind."

"Patience is a virtue."

"Patience sucks."

Laughing, she dressed and smoothed her hair, watching covertly as Alex did the same. His nudity made him appear even more powerful than usual, every inch of him an alpha male.

At last, they were both presentable.

She held out her hands. "One last kiss before we go."

Alex backed away, his expression harried. "I can barely look at you, much less kiss you. Don't be surprised if I drag you behind a palm tree later and take you standing up."

It was hard to tell if he was kidding or not.

Re-dressed in his tux, he was masculine beauty personified. "My prince," she whispered, love squeezing her heart painfully.

His searing gaze swept her from head to toe. "I adore you, Maria. I can't wait to spend the rest of my days with you. You've taken my drab life and added sparkle."

The vulnerability in that statement, coming from a man so big and strong and definitely "unsparkly" made her want to weep. She went to him and wrapped her arms around his waist, laying her head on his shoulder. "I love you."

She felt the muscles in his throat work. He kissed the top of her head. "Let's get this over with, princess. I have plans for you. Big plans…"

Her heart was filled to bursting. Maybe fairy tales did sometimes come true. "Ditto, boss. Anything you say…"

* * * * *

MILLS & BOON®

Why shop at millsandboon.co.uk?

Each year, thousands of romance readers find their perfect read at millsandboon.co.uk. That's because we're passionate about bringing you the very best romantic fiction. Here are some of the advantages of shopping at www.millsandboon.co.uk:

* **Get new books first**—you'll be able to buy your favourite books one month before they hit the shops

* **Get exclusive discounts**—you'll also be able to buy our specially created monthly collections, with up to 50% off the RRP

* **Find your favourite authors**—latest news, interviews and new releases for all your favourite authors and series on our website, plus ideas for what to try next

* **Join in**—once you've bought your favourite books, don't forget to register with us to rate, review and join in the discussions

Visit **www.millsandboon.co.uk**
for all this and more today!